S0-BIN-429

A Despicable Mission
An Olympia Brown Mystery

by

Judith Campbell

Mainly Murder Press, LLC
PO Box 290586
Wethersfield, CT 06129-0586
www.MainlyMurderPress.com

Mainly Murder Press

Editor: Judith K. Ivie
Cover Designer: Karen A. Phillips
Cover Photo: Judith Campbell

All rights reserved

Names, characters and incidents depicted in this book are products of the author's imagination or are used fictitiously. Any resemblance to actual events, organizations, or persons, living or dead, is entirely coincidental and beyond the intent of the author or the publisher.

No part of this book may be reproduced or transmitted in any form or by any means, electronic or mechanical, including photocopying, recording, or by any information storage and retrieval system, without permission in writing from the publisher.

Copyright © 2012 by Judith Campbell
Paperback ISBN 978-0-9836823-9-4
Ebook ISBN 978-0-9846666-6-9

Published 2012 in the United States of America

Mainly Murder Press
PO Box 290586
Wethersfield, CT 06129-0586
www.MainlyMurderPress.com

Dedication

Quite simply, to Chris, my "Professional Englishman," soul mate, singing partner and unsung hero, aggravating editorial nitpicker *par excellence* and best-best friend. And that's the short list. From endless cups of fresh coffee, to silent sea glass walks on White Horse Beach, to arguing over the exact placement of a comma, in so many ways, you make it all happen. So, Kiddo ... this one's for you. Thank you doesn't half say it, but it's the best I've got for now.

Acknowledgments

To my fellow and sister MMP writers, who share this mysterious passion with me, for your generous companionship and encouragement; the 3-on-3 Writers, Vaughn, Melody, Ruthie, Fran, Charlotte, and Jon; the Oak Bluffs Library Writers, Kay, Peggy, Laurel, Barb, Charles, Allen, Iba, Debbie, Andrea, Stephanie, and Else; the British writing contingent, Louise, Steve, Jenny, Gillian, Alex, Annette, Michael, and Abi; to my immediate and extended family, the in-laws, outlaws and bylaws, many of whom appear, not too terribly well disguised, throughout my stories and are still speaking to me; Frimma, David, Deanna, Helene, Jennifer C., and Dan and Nina, my personal cheering section, folks who are "write" there for me on good days and bad; sister author and mentor, Cynthia Riggs, and to the varicolored, diverse, gregarious, and generous people of Martha's Vineyard who give new meaning to the words encouragement, inclusivity, and beloved community. Thank you, thank you, all of you.

**Other Books in the Olympia Brown Mysteries
by Judith Campbell**

A Deadly Mission

An Unspeakable Mission

What They're Saying about the
Olympia Brown Mysteries

The Sinister Minister does it again—a forthright airing of an important social issue.
-- *Cynthia Riggs, author of the Martha's Vineyard, Victoria Trumbull Mystery Series*

If you are a fan of mystery, religion, and psych-thrillers, you will enjoy *A Despicable Mission* by UU minister, Judith Campbell. Protagonist Olympia Brown is a minister who takes the concept of a 24/7 job to new and surprising levels. The cast of characters from her newfound congregation on Martha's Vineyard show the best and worst sides of human behavior. This book is more than a mystery; it is a celebration of human values and liberal religious values in an intimate small town setting.
--*Don Southworth, Executive Director, Unitarian Universalist Ministers Association*

Finding herself in the midst of what appears to be a series of unfortunate accidents involving landed elderly widows belonging to her church, it does not take the ever-inquisitive Olympia Brown long to find herself steeped in the life crises of several members of her congregation. Uncovering the diabolical plot and the characters master-minding these apparent accidents quickly becomes the central focus of Brown's summer ministry and personal mission. In the end we are satisfied with "Mission Accomplished," and yet we are left with enough tantalizing information about Rev. Olympia's ongoing personal relationships to leave the reader looking forward with great anticipation to Campbell's next installment. Olympia Brown is an enjoyable companion with whom to pass a lazy afternoon.

--Rev. Robert Hensley, Rector, Grace Episcopal Church, Martha's Vineyard.

Judith Campbell ... combines the beautiful island setting of Martha's Vineyard with a suspense-filled mystery and emerges with another winner. ...[The third Olympia Brown mystery] *A Despicable Mission* displays Campbell's real talent ... at creating those underlying sub-plots and, in this installment, there are several. Add to this her usual cast of colorful characters and her ever-present house ghost, Ms. Leanna Faith Winslow, and trust me, you won't be disappointed!

--Brenda Scott, Manchester Contemporary Literature Examiner, Examiner.com

Prologue

November 19, 1860

Where to begin? It has been almost four months since I have written anything in these most personal and private pages. And in that time, my whole life has changed. I am carrying a child who will never know its father and am sworn to keep his secret to the grave. I am determined to keep this child and thus will go and stay with my beloved Aunt Louisa until my time is come. Lest I cause alarm by simply disappearing without a trace, I told one or two close friends who knew of my interest in religion that I planned to go off to the city of Cambridge for an extended Christmas holiday. I also said that during that time I would approach the deacons at Harvard College and inquire as to whether I might be allowed to attend some classes there and pursue my interest in theology.

There is some truth in this as I do one day plan to further my education. I promised that once I was settled in I would surely write and tell of my adventures. But what will I write? What can I write? At present all this and more remains a mystery. So far I have managed to conceal my condition with the heavy wraps and shawls that we New Englanders must wear to guard against the cold. But I know I must leave soon.

I've made my choice, and with God and Aunt Louisa's help, I'm determined to see this through. And even as I write these words, a little hand or foot, I know not which, pushes up against my heart as if to underscore this promise and the words I write.

More anon, LFW

One

Mary Elgin Parker, suddenly at home. Arrangements are incomplete at this time. A full obituary will appear in next week's issue of The Martha's Vineyard Times.

"Two never goes without three." Julia Scott-Norton refolded the newspaper and placed it on the wood plank table between them. She and one of her bridge ladies, Sharon McGrath, were enjoying a gossipy girl's lunch at the Black Dog Tavern. Sharon was carefully dissecting a lobster roll, taking out the celery and lining up the bits along the edge of her plate.

"What do you mean?" she asked.

Julia settled into her story. "I mean that Mary Parker is the second elderly person to die alone at home in as many weeks. Maybe I'm being superstitious, but from my experience bad news always comes in threes. Mary Parker and the other one, Doug Bourke, were both getting on in years and determined to stay in houses far too big for them." Julia paused for effect. "And *both* of them died as the result of a fall. Doug slipped getting into the bathtub, and Mary fell down the cellar stairs."

Sharon rested her chin on the palm of her hand and nodded sympathetically. "I know we're all going to die, but think about it, alone and crumpled in a heap on a cement floor. Poor thing, it must have been awful. I know it sounds gruesome, but was it instant, or did she lie there and suffer?"

Julia frowned and shook her head. "Either nobody knows, or nobody's talking. I do know it was a while before somebody found her. I hear they'll be doing an autopsy. I guess it's mandatory with an unattended death, and that means the funeral won't be for a while yet."

Julia paused and smiled. "Remember how she loved wearing those big blowsy hats and going out to lunch? That woman could eat like a horse and run up a flight of stairs like a squirrel. I could never keep up with her. It's hard to believe someone as spry as that could die in a fall. She was full of energy, but at the same time, she was always careful where she put her feet. That's what's so odd about it. It's not like her."

"Is that that summer minister of yours going to do the funeral? Nothing like total immersion starting on day one." Sharon chuckled at her own somewhat obscure baptismal joke.

Julia nodded and tucked a paper napkin into the top buttonhole of her flowered blouse. "I called her and told her about it. Her name's Olympia Brown. She's never been on Martha's Vineyard before, and the first thing we hit her with is a funeral for an island icon with a whole lot of questions surrounding the death."

"Did I hear something about the title to the house being in question as well? My husband Timmy works at the town hall. He said he heard some vague mutterings about it."

"Didn't take long for that to get around, did it?" said Julia.

"It's a small island," said her bridge partner, spearing a juicy pink chunk of lobster.

"Too small sometimes, and that's only one of the questions."

Sharon raised an eyebrow, lowered her voice and peered over her glasses. "What are you saying?"

Julia pushed aside her plate, leaned across the table, and lowered her voice. "I'm saying that some people think it's possible that Mary Parker's death might not have been an accident."

"What about Doug Bourke?" asked Sharon. "He lived alone and died in an accidental fall in the bathtub."

"He really did drown. At least that's what my sister said. She was at the hospital when they brought him in."

"It's tough to get old," said Sharon.

"We don't have much choice," said Julia, holding up an expository index finger, "but from my perspective, it certainly beats the alternative!"

Two

The Rev. Olympia Brown was lying flat on the floor, trying to pry a glowering cat out from under the bed with a broom. She had already secured Thunderfoot, the larger and dumber of the two felines. But Whitefoot, the wily older one, had vanished the minute she saw the cat carrier. With departure time imminent, Olympia was resorting to desperate measures. If all else failed, she'd get out the vacuum cleaner. As luck would have it, the broom, a few dark threats, and a hand full of kitty treats persuaded the wary, flat-eared tortoise-shell into the open and ultimately into the travel cage.

Earlier that year Olympia had accepted the offer of an eight-week position as a summer minister in an historic chapel on the island of Martha's Vineyard. It was going to be a chance to try her hand at parish ministry, which in her current thinking could be the next chapter of her professional life. She knew all about Martha's Vineyard. At least she thought she did, but never until this minute had she envisioned herself as part of that community. Now it was being handed to her on a silver platter, and the ungrateful animals had the audacity to complain. But, standing beside the untidy pile by the door, she asked herself, *do I really need to take all of this? It's not as if Martha's Vineyard is a third world country. They do have electricity and indoor plumbing ... but you never know until you get there what might happen and what you might need.*

The plan was that Frederick Watkins, her recently established live-in English gentleman, would accompany her to the ferry and then come down and join her on weekends when he could. Father Jim Sawicki, her best friend and clergy colleague, had promised to come down and visit for a couple of days as well. She looked at her watch as Frederick crashed through the kitchen door and skidded to a stop at her side. He was sweaty and dirt-streaked from a morning in the garden, and sweet as he was, at that precise moment he was not a thing of beauty.

"Ready, Madame? Your carriage awaits. I just need a quick wash."

"The carriage isn't loaded yet, Frederick. If you take the suitcases, I'll get the box of books. Once those are in, if you'll get the cats, I'll take my clerical robe and lay it on top of everything so it won't wrinkle."

"How in the world are you going to get all of this on the boat, Olympia? Well, actually, I'm going to help with that, am I not?" Frederick had answered his own question. He did that.

"I'm worried about how I'm going to get it all back off. The woman who is my contact, Julia Scott-Norton, said she would be there to meet me. So I guess I'll let her figure it out."

When Olympia's ancient and honorable VW van was loaded, she dashed back for one final check and grabbed the canvas carryall she'd left beside her favorite chair. Earlier in the day she had packed the leather bound diary written by her resident house-ghost, Miss Leanna Faith Winslow, the last descendant of the family to live in the house that was now Olympia's home. She'd been reading that diary in bits ever since she found it the previous

Thanksgiving. It was her personal window on the history of the house and the woman whose grandfather had built it and whose direct ancestor years before him had came over on the Mayflower. Miss Winslow, as Olympia most often referred to her, was a very real and in-your-face ghost. In a moment of absurd reality that only Jim Sawicki and Frederick would understand, she realized she was going to miss, as in think wistfully about, Miss Winslow's nosy intrusions into her daily life. With that thought, she picked up the antique, curved-top wooden clock from its accustomed place on the mantel over the woodstove, blew the dust off it, and stuffed it into the carryall. Now she could leave.

"I'm ready," she said as she pulled herself up into the driver's seat.

"I take it I'm driving back?" said Frederick.

"Is there any another option, my dear?"

Frederick took her right hand in his and held it to his lips. "I'm going to miss you, Olympia. It seems like I only just got here. There's so much I want ..."

Olympia retrieved her hand and made a great show of starting the engine and backing out of the driveway. "Frederick, you'll be joining me in less than a week. I'll have nothing to do there but preach, visit the sick and have tea with elegant Martha's Vineyard ladies. When you do come down we'll have loads of time alone, and we all know that absence makes the heart grow fonder."

"And abstinence makes Freddy a grumpy, dull boy."

"Tighten your seat belt, Frederick, and think of England!"

"What was that? Did I hear a bell or something?

"Must be Miss Winslow's clock," said Olympia. I probably disturbed the mechanism when I stashed it in the back."

"Hmmph," said Frederick. "There it goes again."

Inside Olympia's antique farmhouse the answering machine was recording a message. "This is a message for Reverend Olympia Brown. This is Laura Wilstrom, your daughter. I've decided that I would like to meet you. My cell phone number is 781- 221-7329."

Three

"Life is what happens while you are making other plans."
Olympia first saw those words on a bumper sticker in the
Meriwether College faculty parking lot. She had just
resigned from her position as Professor of Humanities and
college chaplain and found herself thinking about them as
the ferry churned through the whitecaps out of Woods
Hole. The woman who had called her about the job said
that the duties were pretty straightforward: preach on
Sundays, cover pastoral emergencies and be a ministerial
presence in the community. How easy is that? Olympia's
original plan had been to continue the restoration of her
antique farmhouse, get to know Frederick on a
considerably more intimate basis — and think about what
she wanted to do with the rest of her life. Now, feeling
queasy from the rocking of the boat and guilty from
listening to the cats' mounting wails, Olympia hoped that
she'd made the right decision.

When she turned in her last set of grades and said
farewell to her professorial colleagues at her retirement
luncheon, the island job offer seemed like a gift from
heaven. That very same night Julia Scott-Norton, chair of
the governing board of the chapel, called her and painted
an idyllic scene of crayon-colored gingerbread cottages,
Wednesday night hymn sings in the campground, and
sun-swept beaches. The chapel, she said, was a historic

treasure, almost two hundred years old, and it still had its original unpainted wooden doors and pews.

It certainly sounded like the opportunity of a lifetime, eight weeks serving a congregation of forty or fifty people on the fabled island of Martha's Vineyard. She could do it with one hand tied behind her back, and in the abundance of free time they had promised her, she would have enough time to read more of that diary and think through a considerable number of personal options.

First and foremost on that list was her estranged daughter Laura. She had given birth to Laura thirty-five years ago and, under pressure from her mother, given her up for adoption. Only recently, Laura had contacted her through the Department of Records, saying she was pregnant and asking if there was anything in her medical history that might be of concern to her or the unborn child. Olympia wrote back saying that there was nothing that she was aware of and telling her daughter how very much she would like to see her. To that she added that she loved her, and not a day passed that she didn't think about her. She included her Brookfield address and phone number, saying that more than anything in the world, she wanted to reconnect with her in whatever way would be most appropriate for them both. That was in April, and she'd heard nothing since. The waiting was agony.

Also in the succession of midlife options was the little detail of her professional career. This summer would tell her if parish ministry was going to be a serious consideration or not. And then there was Frederick. She'd met him the previous summer, and since that time, their growing relationship had taken several favorable turns. He was a wonderful man, and she was pretty sure she might be thinking about, possibly considering, falling in love with him … maybe.

There was no doubt that he had marriage in mind, but she wasn't even about to let him mention the word. Not now, anyway. He wasn't exactly on the back burner. More like a really good soup, fine wines, and single malt whiskeys, all of which took a long time to mature, Frederick was on slow simmer and coming along nicely.

"Life is what happens while you are making other plans."

On the top deck of the ferry, not fifty feet away from where Olympia was making soothing noises to the cats, two people, looking for all the world like tourists on a day trip, were standing in the lee of the rumbling smoke stack. They were deep in a conversation that was completely and conveniently inaudible to anyone who might pass by. Alden Francis was shading his eyes against the brilliant mid-day sun as he talked to Mary Beth Lessing, an angular, sandal-shod woman standing next to him.

"What about the paperwork, MB? How does it look to you?"

Mary Beth held up a canvas tote bag with Martha's Vineyard blazoned in pink and green across the front and made a circle with her thumb and forefinger.

"It's perfect. Nobody will question it, and not a minute too soon, either. Looks like we're ready to roll on this one."

Al Francis rubbed his chin. He needed a shave. "I still think we're pushing our luck with this one. It's too close to the other one—too many parallels someone could pick up on."

"Ordinarily I'd agree with you,"' said Mary Beth, "but Bateson assures me that this one's dead ripe and ready to fall. Said she's eating out of his hand. Just a matter of signing these papers I've got in here, and we're off on the next ferry."

"I hope you're right, but no matter how you see it, I think we're cutting it a little too close."

"You worry too much. Bateson knows what he's doing. So do you. We'll disappear and lay low after this one until we decide where to, uh, relocate. We're in the business, remember? This is what we do."

"Until our luck runs out."

Mary Beth shook her head. "That's where I disagree with you. I'm the X-factor that no one's looking for. No one expects a woman to be involved in anything like this. Remember, I'm the elder affairs lawyer. At least I play one on television. I give lectures on how to manage finances in your golden years. I wear the white hat, come in at the end and solve everyone's problems."

"And then get the hell out of there before dawn breaks over old Marblehead."

"Something like that."

"It's just that the last one didn't go exactly according to plan."

"It damn sure didn't, but it wasn't my fault. She wasn't supposed to break her neck. That really was an accident."

The two swayed with the motion of the ferry as it made the final turn into the harbor towards the slip. Mary Beth shaded her eyes and looked toward the shore. "I'm going to miss this place. It's really pretty here."

"Tough place to find a drink though," said Al.

Four

On the mezzanine deck Olympia watched through a salt-flecked window as the ferry chummed along. The day was travel brochure perfect, not too hot with a light breeze coming off a green-blue sea that was flashing sparkles of sunlight in all directions. Olympia would have preferred to be topside, but in deference to the cats she remained seated next to them. Her mind was racing ahead of the wind as she wondered how in heaven she was going to get all of her baggage off the boat, and if people from the church would remember to come and meet her, and what the guest cottage she would be staying in would be like, and finally … what would she have for lunch?

She was startled out of her thoughts by a flat voice coming out of a crackly loudspeaker, telling car drivers to return to their vehicles and which side the foot passengers would be disembarking. Olympia stood to see which way the crowd was moving and wishing she remembered which side was port and which was starboard when a voice behind her said, "You wouldn't be Reverend Olympia Brown would you?"

Olympia turned to see a tall, suntanned woman standing behind her, smiling all over in welcome and holding out a large freckled hand. Olympia took the woman's hand and said, "I'm Olympia Brown, but how did you know?"

"It's a small island," said the woman, slinging one of Olympia's bags over her shoulder and scooping up both cat carriers. "I'm Leigh Mayhew; I'm a member of the church you're coming to. We've heard all about you, right down to the cats, Thunderfoot and Whitefoot, yes?"

"That's them," said Olympia, picking up the remaining bags and extending the handle on the mega-suitcase she'd found in a local thrift shop. She looked around herself and wondered just how small this island was going to be.

"Were you on the boat all this time?" she asked.

"Topside," said Leigh, moving toward an exit sign. "You always meet someone you know on this thing. We got talking. When I came down the stairs and saw this woman with a pile of luggage and two cats, I knew it had to be you. Next time, put your suitcases on the cart."

"Cart?" asked Olympia, trying to negotiate the aisle with her load.

"There's a baggage cart for walk-on passengers." Leigh spoke over her shoulder and led the charge as the two women swayed and bumped their way into the line of passengers shuffling towards the debarkation door.

"Do you know the people who are going to meet me and where I'm staying?" Olympia hoped she could be heard over the chatter of the passengers.

"Julia Scott-Norton's in charge of that," said Leigh, hiking one of the sliding bags back up on her shoulder. "She's super organized. She'll be there waiting for you. No need to worry." She paused. "The other member of the welcoming committee is William Bateson."

Leigh dropped her voice and leaned toward Olympia. "He's relatively new. He joined the church a couple months ago and got into the swing of things right from the start. A little too quick for my taste—but then, I'm an old Yankee, and we take generations to do anything."   She rolled her eyes and laughed at her own joke.

The exit door opened, and the crowd moved as a single body in the direction of fresh air.   Olympia walked close beside Leigh so she could hear her companion over the surrounding chatter.

"He's helpful, but he's everywhere at once, if you get my drift."

Olympia thought she did but offered no comment.

"He fusses over the old ladies," said Leigh, walking carefully on the sharply inclined ramp. "Actually, I think he might be gay. You know the type, affected and kind of flirty and attentive. Anyway, they all love it. I guess he's OK, just not my style. Too much, too quick for my island reserve. We like to take a little longer in getting to know people. Habit, I guess."

Again Olympia made no comment. She headed out the exit door with her overload of baggage and Leigh chattering on like they had known each other for years.

"There they are," she said, indicating with a nod of her head. "William is the one with the flowers, and Julia's the woman beside him with the wraparound sunglasses."

Olympia spotted them, lifted her chin and smiled. Waving was totally out of the question. She stayed as close as she could to Leigh and picked her way carefully down the passenger ramp to her welcoming committee of two. Behind her deliberately eager smile, she was hoping this had been a wise decision. But now, walking down the plank, there was no turning back. It was too late for second thoughts. In those last few moments before she set foot on the island of Martha's Vineyard for the very first time, she ran her fingers through her windblown hair, patted it into place and hoped she was putting her best foot forward. She looked out at the multicolored assemblage of people gathered around the base of the exit ramp and realized that she had no idea what she was getting herself into.

But really Olympia, isn't all of life a mystery? You're a minister, for God's sake, what did you expect? And with that scrap of philosophic self-assurance, Olympia took a deep breath and stepped forward to join them.

Five

November 26, 1860
I feel such a stranger here. The crowded streets and red brick buildings of Cambridge, Massachusetts are a long way and a far cry from the little town I left behind. But I have come here because I need time to think and to prepare for a life I could not have imagined a year ago. God bless my stalwart and progressive aunt. Without her, this would have been so much more difficult...but not impossible.
More anon, LFW

Leigh Mayhew steered Olympia though a shifting sea of overheated men and women, barking dogs, sticky children and bulging suitcases. When they cleared the crowd she introduced her to Julia Scott-Norton, a pewter haired woman who could have been in her middling fifties, and William Bateson, a man who was slightly shorter than Julia, impeccably dressed and holding a coffee can full of beach roses and wild daisies.

"Here, let me help you with those things," said William, taking the roller-suitcase handle out of Olympia's hands and replacing it with the flowers. Julia Scott-Norton relieved Leigh of one of the cat carriers and immediately began making cat-comforting noises to the wide-eyed captives. Olympia smiled gratefully, sniffed at the flowers and promptly sneezed.

"Oh, dear," said William "I hope you're not allergic. These things grow all over the island. If they bother you, you're going to have a hard time."

"Nope, just the salt air and change of temperature. I'll be OK in a minute." Olympia smiled and sniffed the flowers a second time to prove her point.

Julia took command without ever saying a word, and in a few well-organized minutes, the four of them were trooping through the parking lot toward a dusty green minivan. Leigh waved an energetic farewell, saying she'd see them at the pot-luck that night, and she hoped Olympia would like the cottage, and she was so glad she was here and …

Pot luck tonight? But what about …

Olympia said nothing, trusting that all would be made clear in due time. Distance and passing cars obliterated the rest of Leigh's enthusiastic verbal stream of consciousness, and she climbed into the car. Olympia smiled and waved. That woman could talk, but even in those few moments it was clear she had a heart as big as she was tall, and she wore it high on her sleeve for all to see.

Olympia squashed herself into the middle seat of the van and sat with an uneasy cat on either side of her. William took the passenger seat next to Julia and then looked back over his shoulder to check on her. When they were buckled in, Julia started the engine, eased out of the waiting area into a slowly moving line of traffic, and immediately began the orientation tour. She had a lovely low, clear speaking voice.

"This is five corners," she said over her shoulder, "the land of restaurants, rental agencies and the occasional protest demonstration and peace rally. I'll get us through it as best I can, but from the end of May until the end of September, it's a madhouse." She turned back and laughed. "I tell people the only way to get through is to shut your eyes and step on it."

Olympia hoped she was joking but didn't know Julia well enough to ask. Once they were through the intersection, she turned right onto the main street of Vineyard Haven. Looking back and forth through the open windows, Olympia took in as much as she could and within minutes was on visual overload. The place was sweet and colorful, like stepping into a candy house at Christmas time. After a few more lefts and rights which entirely did in Olympia's sense of direction, Julia turned onto West Maple Street and pulled over in front of a little house that seemed to be growing out of the larger dwelling next to it. It wasn't much bigger than a garage, and soon Olympia would learn that was exactly how it started out. She would also learn that just about anything that could be made into a living space or a rental unit was soon converted. Life was expensive on the island, and affordable rentals were at a premium.

William waved his hand in the direction of the diminutive purple and white cottage.

"Here you are, Reverend Brown, home sweet dollhouse. Or as we say in the real estate business, quaint and cozy, which further translates into tiny. It used to be a two-car garage with a door connecting to the main house. Eudora West, she's the owner, put up a couple of walls, added a kitchenette and a broom closet that passes for a bathroom, and voila! A guest house. She lets the church use it if she isn't renting it." He lowered his voice to a more confidential tone. "She's getting on, though, might not be able to do it too much longer. She wanted to come and meet you, but she'd made other plans. You'll love her. She's a real sweetheart, isn't she Julia?"

"I'm looking forward to it." Olympia leaned forward to open the mini-van door, but William Bateson was fast ahead of her. In one motion he'd opened the passenger door and picked up a cat carrier while she was still fumbling with her seat belt. Once unbuckled, she picked up her other cat carrier and walked up a weed-sprinkled brick path to her new home away from home.

Julia stepped between the two of them, opened the grape colored door and stood to one side so Olympia could be the first to go in. It smelled like it had been closed up for a while, not musty or moldy, just very much in need of an open window or two or three and a good, stiff breeze.

William Bateson set down his cat carrier inside the door and began describing the place to Olympia. "It is small, but I think you'll find it has everything, including a teeny second bedroom which you might want to use for an office. You even have a fenced-in yard for the felines. Without saying a word, Julia took William's arm and turned him around, stopping him mid-spiel. "Come on. We'll go out for the rest of her things. That way she can have a little look around for herself."

"But I thought I might ..."

Julia smiled and moved him toward the door.

Olympia chuckled at the interchange and made a mental note of it as she turned back to look at the home that the generous Mrs. West had so graciously offered her. Julia was right, it did seem to have everything a person could need and most of it within arm's reach. The design was clever and made good use of every available inch. Olympia took a deep breath, counted to ten and went to oversee the rest of the unloading.

Once all of the bags and boxes were inside, Julia gave her a quick inventory.

"The futon sofa here opens to a double bed, if you need extra sleeping accommodations. You did say you were unmarried, did you not? She looked at Olympia over the top of her glasses.

"I'm not married."

William looked away and fingered his lapel, and Julia started opening windows.

Suddenly Olympia felt very tired. As much as these two were trying to make her feel welcome, she wanted nothing more than to be alone with her cats and settle in to her new digs by herself.

"About the car," she started to say.

"We'll be bringing it by later this afternoon, about five-thirty. You can follow us back to the church for the pot-luck. Don't worry about bringing anything this time. I've already made enough for an army. Vegetarian, eggs and dairy, right?" Julia was now fluffing pillows and straightening curtains.

"Tonight?" said Olympia.

"Everybody in the church wanted to do something to welcome you, and pot-lucks are such an island thing. We told everyone you're vegetarian, so you'll probably have bean sprouts growing out of your ears by the end of your stay here."

Once again Julia laughed at her little joke, and Olympia added another mental note to her list. *Misses nothing!*

"I can stay and help if you'd like." William was nodding his head.

"That's really kind of you, William," said Olympia, "but I've been up since five this morning, and I need to sit down and put my feet up for a while."

"Of course, of course, of course. Silly of me. You need to be alone. Maybe later."

Olympia smiled and covered an exaggerated yawn.

Julia turned toward Olympia but spoke to William.

"I'll meet you out in the car. I just need to speak to The Reverend about some church business."

"Oh, please do call me Olympia. I much prefer it."

"Surely, Olympia. We've had a death over the weekend, an elderly lady named Mary Parker. She was an island character and member of the church, but she didn't come very often. She preferred going out to lunch—said she got more out of it." Julia winked and continued. "Her son hasn't said what they want in terms of a service yet, but he implied there was a problem. It's all rather unclear at the moment. I do think it will be a graveside service rather than something in the chapel. Dan, that's her son, will undoubtedly want to meet with you. I'm hoping you have a cell phone. I'm not sure what the telephone arrangement is in the cottage yet."

Olympia gulped. "Oh, gosh, I left it charging on my dresser at home. I'll have Frederick bring it this weekend."

"Frederick?"

She swallowed a second time. "Um, he's a good friend. He's coming down for the weekend. I'll ask him to bring it with him. So you don't know if there's a working phone in the cottage?" Olympia looked around, trying to see if she could locate one.

"I'm sure there is, but I think it might just be an extension off the main phone in Dory's house. I'll leave any messages with Dory until we've sorted it out."

"Who's Dory?" asked Olympia.

"Eudora West, your landlady." Julia smiled at a confused Olympia. "Sit down and put your feet up. For such a little island, we manage to keep ourselves pretty busy. Try and get some rest before tonight. It will do you a world of good."

Six

When she heard the car drive off, Olympia reached inside the canvas carryall and took out Miss Winslow's clock and diary. These were her connections to home. The wooden case of the clock was warm from being in the sun. She looked around for a good place to put it and finally decided on a painted wooden bookcase on the far wall across from the front door. That way she would see it first thing when she came in, as well as from the chair by the window where she planned to do more than a little reading.

With that accomplished, she set up the cats with food and their litter box and left the cautious beasties to settle in while she explored the rest of the cottage for herself.

The larger, brighter bedroom was just big enough for a standard double bed and maybe one book, if she didn't open it up all the way. She and Frederick would be in close company when he visited, but Olympia didn't see that as a problem.

The kitchen had all the necessaries, only in miniature, and the shower in the bathroom had been designed for a very thin person.

Olympia retrieved the flowers from where William had left them and set them on the window sill behind the sink. In so doing she found a business card propped against the screen.

The Gingerbread Man
William F. Bateson
Prime Vineyard Properties
Sales, Rentals, Property Management

Olympia picked up the card and turned it over. On the back there was short note and a different telephone number. "If you are ever interested in owning property here, please call me at this number."

Interesting.

From these multiple first impressions, it was likely that this assignment might be considerably busier than she had originally anticipated. On the other hand it would be a different kind of busy from the academic world, and that's what she was looking for. Surely a pot-luck or two and a few church services, add a funeral to that, and the odd cup of tea with an elderly landlady would still leave time to relax, touch up her résumé and think about the future. *Exactly what future, and with whom shall I share it?*

She tried not to dwell on the subject of her distant daughter, but ever since she had received the letter saying Laura was pregnant and asking about Olympia's medical history, even including a photograph, Olympia had begun to hope that this personal agony might one day be resolved.

She stretched her arms over her head, arched her back and dropped into the armchair beside the window. Alone in the warm quiet of her temporary new home, she was staring at the pattern cast on the tabletop by the sunlight coming through the lace curtain when she was startled back into the present by the sound of knocking behind her. Unwillingly, she pulled herself up out of the comfort and solitude of the chair and the sunshine and opened her front door to a diminutive older lady holding out a plate of cookies.

She inclined her head slightly as she introduced herself. "Good afternoon, Reverend Brown, I'm Eudora West, your landlady."

Olympia's mother would have described her as being no bigger than a minute, and it would have been an accurate description. The woman standing at the door was all of five feet tall. Her light brown skin and short-cropped, tightly curled white hair bespoke her African-American ancestry. She was wearing a pink and blue madras plaid skirt and a light blue blouse, and she had a pink sweater over her narrow shoulders. A pink flowered cane hung over her right wrist.

"May I come in and tell you about the house?"

"Oh, please. I'm not really moved in yet, but there isn't that much to unpack. Looks like you've thought of everything I'll ever need. It's lovely. Here, let me get you a chair."

Olympia glanced at the cane.

"Just for balance," said Eudora West.

"Of course, Mrs. West, I was hoping I would have a chance to meet you before I have to go back out. William Bateson told me that you own the house."

Eudora walked into the room, set the cookies on the table and settled herself in the window chair. Olympia cleared a place for herself on the futon and sat facing her first guest.

"Do please call me Dory, and may I call you Olympia? Mr. West died years ago, poor dear, and even when he was alive, I never did like being Mrs. Anyone. The name

Eudora sounds like the hostess at a snooty white lady's garden party. And just for the record, what else did Mr. William Bateson tell you about me?"

"Not much of anything other than you wanted to meet me and you were probably napping when we arrived."

Olympia looked toward the kitchen and started to get up. "I'd make you some tea or something, but I don't know what's here. I'll need to go shopping. Would you like a glass of water?"

"Sit down, dear. I can get water if I need it. I know where it is. Let me tell you about the house and see if you have any questions about where things are and how they work."

Dory ended her sentence with a half-smile and an upward lift of her chin. It was a charming and endearing gesture, and in that moment Olympia fell completely in love with this tiny, intelligent, fiercely independent wisp of a woman.

After they had gone over the particulars of the house with a little bit of island history and gossip thrown in for good measure, Dory gave Olympia directions to the nearest grocery store, which was less than a ten-minute walk from the house.

"I usually have cup of tea about this time of day, Olympia, if ever you'd like to come next door and join me."

"That's an invitation I won't refuse. It just so happens I have an English gentleman friend who's been educating me on the time-honored custom of afternoon tea. I'll try and find some of my favorite teas while I'm shopping. Maybe you'd like to try some."

"English gentleman friend?" Dory winked broadly. "I do hope you'll introduce me when he comes to visit. I had an English friend once. I just love their accents."

"That's a promise, Dory. You'll love him."

She held up her right index finger. "If you do, then I'm sure I will."

Olympia closed the door behind her landlady and recalled a not-so-nice cup of tea that had been intended for her almost a year ago. She shuddered and pushed away the thought. That was all behind her now. She was beginning a new life, and this was the first day. Olympia leaned back on the sofa and then shifted the pillows and lifted her legs so she could stretch out for a minute. Then she stretched out a little farther.

~

At home in Brookfield, Frederick was listening to the answering machine and carefully writing down the number that Olympia's daughter left on the tape, but when he tried to call her and heard the cell phone ringing in their shared bedroom, he knew they had a problem. The only number she had given him was the church office number, and who would be there at this hour? Tomorrow he would call and leave a message if Olympia hadn't called him before then.

~

At precisely five-thirty Julia Scott-Norton parked her green minivan outside the door, and right behind her, William Bateson pulled up in an ancient, dusty blue Volvo station wagon. Olympia looked at her watch and opened the door. She had been asleep for almost two hours and suspected she still had pillow creases in her cheek.

Julia waved through the car window, and William got out of the Volvo and walked up the path holding out the keys.

"Can you drive a standard shift?"

Is the pope a Catholic? "I've driven one all my life. They are getting harder to find, though. I'll enjoy it." She accepted the key and asked who she should thank for such an extended courtesy.

"Mary Mayhew, Leigh Mayhew's great aunt. Six or seven generations of Mayhews have been coming to the church. She's the most recent, and she's close to eighty, but for heaven's sake don't tell her I mentioned her age."

Olympia looked out at the boxy old car and wondered which one of those six generations it dated from.

William caught the look and said, "Like the fabled Bostonian ladies who *have* their hats, Reverend, Martha's Vineyard ladies *have* their cars. And let me tell you, a real island car is truly priceless and defies description."

You've got that right.

Olympia nodded politely and walked down the path to where Julia was sitting in her own car. "Feeling more refreshed, Olympia?"

"Not quite yet. Would you mind giving me directions to the church? The day got away from me, and I'd like to have a quick shower and change my clothes before I meet people."

Julia began to describe where the church was located, but before she could finish, William pulled a pen and paper out of his pocket and sketched out a quick map complete with street names and directional arrows. The man was amazing.

"Thanks, I'll be there in two shakes."

Olympia's sudden shyness about meeting and socializing with a group a people she didn't really know came as a surprise. She was used to mingling and making small talk at the college. So where did this come from? But any sense of awkwardness was immediately put to rest as she walked up the wooden steps and stepped into the soft golden light of the knotty pine interior of the chapel. It was beautiful. She was greeted by the sounds of clinking glasses and people in happy conversation. Leigh Mayhew was the first to wave enthusiastically without spilling a drop of whatever she had in her hand.

"I see you've found us. Here, first things first, let me get you something to drink, wine, beer, soda? Then we'll start introducing you around."

"White wine if you have it? I'm really looking forward to meeting you all."

As if by magic, a man wearing chino shorts and a light blue golf shirt materialized out of the crowd and held out a generous glass of something pale and cool and decidedly alcoholic. Olympia sniffed and sipped. It was acceptable.

"And we are looking forward to meeting you, Reverend Brown. For such a little church we seem to have a lot of things going on. I'm Mike Herlihy. I'm the sexton, and my wife Deb is the church administrator."

Olympia turned to the man speaking to her. "Oh, do please call me Olympia. And is this your wife?"

A slender woman with straight, dark blond hair and a wonderful open smile held out her hand. "I'm Deb. I'm only part time here at the church, but I'll do whatever I can to help you settle in."

Before Olympia could respond, William Bateson materialized out of the conversational clusters of people, slipped his arm though hers and led her away.

"My my, Olympia, that was a quick change. Now if you don't mind, let me get everyone's attention, and I'll introduce you."

He clapped his hands a few times, and people turned slowly from their nibbles and with glasses in hand looked expectantly toward the newcomer.

"Ladies and gentlemen, here is our summer minister, Reverend Doctor Olympia Brown. Julia and I collected her and the cats at around mid-day and settled her into Dory West's guest cottage, and now we are celebrating her arrival with one of our incredible community church pot-lucks and her choice of the finest of jug wine."

William waited for the ripple of forced laughter to die down before he continued with his introduction. When he finished they all applauded, made greeting pleasantries and quickly returned to their own conversations.

Olympia thanked him and then walked over to where Julia Scott-Norton was standing apart and observing the festivities.

"Would you mind introducing me to a few people? I feel a bit awkward being new and just barging in on conversations."

Julia looked pleased to be asked and steered Olympia to a group of people standing around the snacks table. As they drew closer she could hear snatches of a conversation about sailing and choppy water and other nautical terms she'd read about. She realized she didn't know thing one about sailing, didn't know the pointy end from the flat end of a boat, the star from the board, the mast from the plank. She did, however, have some familiarity with the significance of the sun being over the yardarm, and with glass in hand, she hoped it might suffice."

"Well, well, and welcome to you, Reverend Olympia. Tell me, do you sail?" A tall sunburned gentleman wearing faded jeans and a short-sleeved white shirt with the mandatory tennis sweater tied over his shoulders extended his free hand.

Olympia took his hand and smiled. "The answer to your question is, I've never been on a sailboat in my life, but I'd love to be asked."

"Well, I'm Jack Winters, and as of right this minute, with witnesses to prove it, consider yourself asked. I hereby invite you to go sailing with us tomorrow or the next day, if you already have plans, and the weather cooperates."

He put an avuncular arm over her shoulders and gave her a friendly squeeze. Olympia didn't like being touched, much less hugged, without permission. They did describe this place as being casual, but how casual is casual? She made herself relax and smile before responding.

"How very kind of you. I would love to take you up on your invitation, but I want to feel my way around the island a little bit. And then of course there is the Sunday service to prepare. Maybe next week or the week after, if I can have a rain check?"

Olympia moved out from under his arm and stepped back to a more comfortable distance as they were joined by a well tanned and slightly flushed woman.

"What about Sunday? "Hi, Olympia, I'm Janney, Mrs. Jack." She gestured to her husband with her thumb. "Be careful of old Jack-in-the-box here, people have been known to disappear for days when he takes them out on that boat of ours. Bring a life jacket, a big stick and plenty of gin." She turned toward the food table. "Now I do believe they are calling us to the trough."

Olympia couldn't say for sure whether it was the unevenness of the wooden plank floor under her feet or the press of people moving toward the extravagant buffet, but she thought for a moment that she saw Janney Winters stagger.

After filling her plate, Olympia found an empty seat at one of the long plank tables and was greeted by welcoming smiles and beckoning gestures and encouragement to try a little bit of everything. When she got up to go back for seconds, Leigh called out and told her to make sure to save room for desserts — plural. The wine and the promise of abundant calories to come were turning this into a very pleasant evening indeed.

By the time she was well into a wedge of strawberry chiffon pie, William Bateson stood and tapped the side of his coffee cup to get everyone's attention. Olympia noted a few shiftings and rollings of eyes as he did so and added this to the growing collection of things to ponder when she got home that night.

When the place grew quiet he made a few housekeeping announcements and then called upon Julia Scott-Norton to say a few words. She looked casually elegant, as so many of the women there did. Tonight she was wearing beige slacks and a yellow linen blouse topped by a long-sleeved beige jacket. She turned and smiled over to where Olympia was sitting before beginning to speak.

"I'm sure a few of you have had a chance speak with Olympia this evening, but there are still many who have not, so I shall be hosting a little tea at my house for just the ladies of the church tomorrow at three in the afternoon."

Olympia glanced over to a frowning Jack Winters, who made an ocean wave action with his right hand and then crossed his two hands in front of his face which she understood to mean they would not be sailing tomorrow. Olympia responded with a slightly regretful smile and a giant internal sigh of relief.

Julia beckoned to Olympia to join her, then asked, "Is there anything you'd like to say before we start clearing up?"

Olympia wasn't so sure she liked being the center of attention, but for now she would go along with what was asked of her. Tomorrow, she wouldn't be so tired, and things wouldn't be quite so new. She patted her lips with a paper napkin and stood.

"Let me start by saying how full I am of all your good food, and thank you so much for respecting my vegetarianism. I'd love to have the recipes."

This was received with several appreciative murmurs, nods and smiles.

"I'll do my best to learn your names, but for the next few days please remind me again when we meet. I'm delighted to be here, and I guess I'll see many of you ladies at tea tomorrow." *So much for a day to myself!*

"So now you know Julia, our lovely president." Olympia turned to find Leigh Mayhew beside her. "She's a real steel magnolia. Tough as nails and good as they come, and she gets things done. I guess she's a mixed blessing. Nobody wanted to be chair of the board, too political." Leigh leaned closer and dropped her voice. "Too many secrets and too many skeletons in the island closet, but don't tell anyone I told you. I'll see you at tea at precisely three in the afternoon."

Then she winked, held up her hands and whispered. "For the record, I'm not wearing white gloves, and I'm unsure whether I'll even wear a bra. I will, however, wear a big untidy hat."

With that, Leigh was up and gone, and Olympia was left trying to stifle a fit of giggles and wondering what in heaven, or hell, this place was really like and what kind of an adventure would be in the learning of it.

~

Alone in the empty antique farmhouse in Brookfield, Frederick was putting together his own version of supper: a room-temperature bottle of beer, a slab of overripe cheddar that smelled like an old sock, and two slices of homemade bread, followed by a second beer. This was not how he had envisioned his summer, but life happens, and you damn the torpedoes and get on with it, don't you? At least that's what his red-haired mother had said when he whined about something. Even though Olympia was separated from him by thirty or so land miles and seven water miles, she was still one hell of a lot closer than she was when he was in England. He would surely get in touch with her tomorrow, and if he finished up in the garden, maybe he'd surprise her and come down a day or two sooner.

The house was suddenly too big and too quiet for the gentle man from England. To counter it, he turned on the radio and found some classical music, but it was far from being enough to fill the void.

Seven

Olympia tried calling Frederick when she got up the next morning. When he didn't answer, she left a message saying that she was calling from an extension in her cottage and didn't have a call-back number yet but would call him as soon as she did. Oh, yes, and she missed him. *She really missed him.*

After that, she put away a few things and then walked into Vineyard Haven to check out a local book store called, of all things, Bunch of Grapes. When she got back home, a few dollars poorer and a few books richer, she had just enough time to set up her laptop on the table in front of the window before it was time to go to tea ... sans hat and white gloves.

Julia Scott-Norton's West Chop house looked like something straight out of a cherished Vineyard scrap book. Old family pieces of wicker and polished mahogany were sitting side by side. Carefully patched and mended chair cushions, glassware and china, no longer in complete sets but lovingly saved and elegantly jumbled together on a wonderful old gate-leg table with a book propping up the back left leg.

An overweight yellow lab lumbered to the door and greeted Olympia. He barked once, sniffed her hand and then leaned his full weight against her, slid down her leg and rolled onto his back in full expectation of the belly-rub which she promptly provided.

"You're a dog lover, I see." Her hostess was beaming approval.

"I've had dogs off and on all of my life, but right now I'm just running around too much to give a dog proper care. It's not fair to the animal to be left alone. Cats are more adaptable."

Julia nudged the blissful pooch with the side of her foot. "Good thinking. Animals are a responsibility. Ours are members of the family. We've got a couple of cats, as well, but they go into hiding when they see the tea cart. Too many people."

Olympia stood and brushed the dog hair off her hands just as several of the women she had seen the night before entered without knocking.

"We all came together so we could save gas and wouldn't have too many people parking on your lawn." Leigh Mayhew led the charge, heading directly for the kitchen. "I made some cucumber sandwiches without crusts, of course. Where do you want me to put them?"

"Oh, you can leave them right on the table here in the dining room. I'll wash off the plastic wrap, and you can take it with you when you go."

Julia had everything orchestrated right down to the recycling. Olympia was impressed with her efficiency but wondered what might be beyond it. She wondered if she would ever find out. Was this outwardly friendly group of people in reality a tightly closed, clannish society that would take generations to include a newcomer? They painted a lovely picture for all to see with their chipped family china and mended heirloom tablecloths and beloved family dogs, but would she or any newcomer ever see beyond what she was seeing today? And if they did, what would they find?

Before Olympia had time to speculate about what else might appear before her wondering eyes, more ladies arrived, deposited their plates on the table and arranged themselves into conversation groups throughout the living room, dining room and out onto the wide, wraparound porch. The big old house seemed to ramble around and almost fold back in upon itself. In some ways it reminded her of her own home back in Brookfield, and she was suddenly swept with a longing for it and for her funny-faced Englishman that left her breathless.

"So how is your second day on our wonderful island?" Janney Winters leaned in so close that Olympia could smell cigarette smoke and peppermint on her breath.

"I'm still settling in. My little house is darling—well, teeny really, but it's all I need."

"We're so glad the place is working out for you," said Jeanne, whose last name she'd forgotten since the night before. "Some of us were afraid it might be too small."

Olympia took a plate and layered it with cucumber sandwiches and assorted cookies. "As long as I have a place to write and sleep, food for the cats and a cup of tea or a glass of wine in their proper sequence, I'm fine. The rest can be worked out."

"You can come over for a glass of wine with me anytime you want," said Janney companionably—too companionably. *There was the peppermint smell again.*

Olympia saw the glances and decided on the spot that the last thing she was likely do would be to drink wine with Janney Winters and very little with anyone else for that matter. Didn't Leigh Mayhew say only yesterday that this was a small island? Olympia was beginning to understand there wasn't much privacy here, but was that a good thing or a bad thing? A close-knit community could be very supportive. It could also strangle you.

For the rest of the afternoon, Olympia and the ladies made pleasant conversation around subjects of the church, its history, and the problems that come along with a historic building that needs work but no one wants to alter in any way. They were, in fact, providing her with a loving and proud picture of their church and their community. If there were tensions, they were not in evidence around the tea table.

The conversation turned to this and that, and as the sandwiches and cookies dwindled to a precious few, the women began to trickle out. Julia started clearing up, and Olympia pitched right in, consolidating sandwiches and compatible cookies onto plates and looking around for some plastic wrap she could re-use.

Julia held out a crumpled handful. "You learn fast. You'll do well here. I'm so glad you could come."

"Come today, or come here to the church?"

"Both, I guess, but mostly I mean today. Do you have to leave right away?" She was brushing the last of the crumbs into her hand and tossing them out the door for the birds. "I'd like to fill you in a little more on the ins and outs of the church and the island. You got a pretty good idea of who we are and what we look like this afternoon, but we both know there's more than meets the eye anywhere you go."

"I've got time," said Olympia.

Julia got them each one more cup of tea, and they settled themselves onto a pair of painted wooden rockers that faced out to the sea. *It really is like the pictures in the travel guides,* thought Olympia, rocking back and forth and sipping her tea. *The big porch, the distant view of the harbor, a soft breeze coming off the water, and nowhere to be but here. I could get used to this.*

Julia broke into her thoughts. "I wanted to talk to you alone because I have some concerns about something that might be going on, but I'm not sure, and I don't know how to find out."

Olympia leaned forward, wondering what in heaven was coming next.

"Julia lowered her voice. "One of the reasons I'm even telling you this is because it involves your landlady, Dory West. If there is some monkey business afoot, you are in a better position than most of us to keep an eye on her."

"I don't understand, is she ill or something?"

"Oh, heavens no, just the opposite. She's getting older and more frail, but her health is OK. No, this is something else. Ever since her husband died, she's been talking about selling the house. For the last ten years she's been saying it was getting too much for her. I don't think she really wants to sell it; I think she just likes to fuss now and then, and the house is as good a thing to fuss over as anything else. She loves the place. I always thought she'd stay until she was carried out. Now I'm not so sure."

The discomfort in Julia's voice was evident.

"She came over for a visit yesterday, right after you and William left," said Olympia. "She even brought me some homemade cookies and said if I needed anything I should come right over. She seemed pretty capable to me."

"She is capable and sharp as a tiny little tack, but of late, something seems to have changed."

Olympia sipped her cooling tea. "I don't know her at all, but after ten years of being on her own, maybe it really is getting to be too much. Does she have any family?"

"She has one daughter who lives in Washington State. She doesn't see her all that often, but she calls regularly. Dory's eighty-four, and she still goes out to see her at least once a year. Of course, she comes back here every spring before the tourists get here."

Julia finished her tea and set her cup and saucer down on the floor beside her rocker. "I think what might be bothering me ... is William Bateson. You met him yesterday. I'm not sure, but I think he might be pushing her to sell and let him handle the sale. He says he works for an island realty company, and I think he might be looking for business. Dory's place is a prime piece of property. It's in a lovely West Chop neighborhood, it's a nice solid house plus the guest house, and it's walking distance to town. She would get a very good price, but I don't think she really wants to sell. Dory hasn't said anything to me, but the fact that she's no longer talking about selling set me to thinking."

"About what?"

Julia leaned closer to Olympia. "Ever since William Bateson started coming to church, he's been very attentive to her. Half the people there think he's gay, the way he fusses over her and some of the other older women."

"I thought he was your friend."

Julia spoke with a sharpness in her voice that Olympia hadn't heard before. "The devil you know is better than the devil you don't. I don't know what he's up to or even if he's up to anything at all. If he thinks I'm his friend, I can learn a lot more about him than if he thinks I don't like him. That's why I keep asking him to help out with things around the church. Like I said, right now it's just an uneasy feeling, and I could be a hundred and eighty degrees off the mark."

Olympia hesitated. She wasn't quite sure how to respond. Nothing like this had ever been discussed in seminary, and she was feeling distinctly uncomfortable. She wished she could ask Jim or Frederick what to do, but she was here on her own and very much at sea in more ways than one. *Keep it noncommittal, Olympia.*

"Um-m-m, what exactly did you have in mind?"

"If you don't mind, for now just keep an eye on his comings and goings next door, maybe find a reason to pop in when he's there. You know, ask for a cup of sugar or something. Then if you notice anything or even sense anything that might be amiss, I'm asking you to tell me. This isn't exactly in your job description, but I don't know who else to ask. I have absolutely no evidence; it's a feeling, and a very uncomfortable one at that. The man is a newcomer. He doesn't know the island way of doing things. Dory is getting older, and she lives alone in that big old house. Like I said, it's a feeling, but it's strong enough that I wanted to tell someone who is not an islander, but someone I felt I could trust."

Olympia wondered if she should tell her about finding Bateson's business card on her windowsill and then thought better of it. It was too early in all of this to take sides. She would hold back and give Mr. William Bateson the benefit of the doubt. It was clear that Julia liked being in charge of things. *She is, after all, president of the board.* Maybe she was resentful of this newcomer-interloper trying to move into her territory? Such things were not unknown or uncommon in small, tightly knit communities. Didn't Leigh Mayhew tell her that islanders were a friendly lot, but they liked to take their time about it?

Eight

Driving home from Julia Scott-Norton's tea party, Olympia had a lot to think about before Sunday, and very little of it seemed to do with ministry. *On the other hand, maybe it has everything to do with ministry. Talk about a rapid learning curve.* She was already driving more confidently and by five in the afternoon was thinking about supper. She wondered what might be available in the local market in terms of a no-cook, low impact meal for herself and the cats.

When she turned into the crowded parking lot, it appeared that half the population of the island must have had the same idea, and she had to circle twice before she found a space. Conveniently, someone had left an empty shopping cart in front of her car, but as she made a dive for it, she heard someone calling her name.

"Olympia! Olympia, is that you? Over here."

She turned in the direction of the voice and saw Jack and Janney Winters weaving through the parked cars toward her. There was no escape.

"Hey, there," said Olympia with a bonhomie she did not feel. "This really is a small island. I've only been here for a day, and already I'm meeting people I know."

"Didn't think I'd see you so soon," said Janney, linking her arm through Olympia's. "We stopped to pick up some things for supper." Janney lowered her voice to a more confidential level and patted her chest. "That was a lovely party this afternoon, but I wish Julia had served something besides tea. I was dry as a bone when I got out of there. Between you and me, Dearie, Mrs. Julia Scott-Norton the Third may have a blood line as long as your arm, but she sure can't make a drink!"

"I'll bet you're going to get something for supper, too. That right Olympia?" Jack caught hold of her free arm. "Why don't you follow us back to the boat and have supper with us? We've plenty of food, don't we, honey? Maybe even go for a little sunset sail. Howzzat sound?"

It sounds like I'm trapped.

"I need to get food for the cats. They'll never forgive me, and, well, I was planning on working on my sermon. You know, as in Sunday morning?" Olympia offered a hopeful glance.

Jack released her arm as they neared the door. "OK, quick supper with us, and no sailing tonight. You'll still have time for the sermon. Hell, we might even come hear you. Whadadya think, Janney? You like variety." Jack looked over the top his sunglasses at his wife. "Going to church on a Sunday morning would certainly be a change for you." Jack was laughing at his own joke, but the barb was evident under the laughter.

Olympia felt a sense of semi-reprieve. "OK. Why don't I pick up some ice cream for dessert then? I can feed the cats when I get home. It's really very kind of you."

When they'd finished shopping, Olympia said she would follow them in her own car and asked exactly where she was going.

"Oak Bluffs Harbor," Jack boomed and pointed off to his right. "That way. We have a mooring right against the sidewalk. Comes in handy for entertaining. Great little spot for drinks and dining *al fresco*."

Jack shaded his eyes against the afternoon sun and raised an eyebrow when he said the words *al fresco*. "I'll drive slowly; I wouldn't want to lose you."

The sexual overtone in his last comment was unmistakable. Olympia was sure she wasn't imagining it, and she damn sure didn't like it, but it was too late to back out now.

By the time she located a parking space and found the Winters' boat, Janney already had a drink in her hand and was enthusiastically waving Olympia aboard. She had never been on a pleasure boat before, and despite her initial discomfort at being pressured into being there, she was fascinated by the way the craft was constructed, how every little convenience had been thought of and provided. On either side of the *Janney-Lee*, Olympia saw people doing much the same as they were, setting up cocktail party arrangements that connected the sitting area on the back of the boats and the sidewalk along the harbor. One family even put out plastic palm trees and pink flamingoes along with the onion dip and the chips. Olympia relaxed her cautious reserve a notch. This was just too public for anything uncomfortable to happen.

Jack bowed and held out a wine glass. "Something cool and pale for the lady minister. I seem to remember you had white wine at our pot luck supper last night. I think you'll find this a tad better than the el cheapo stuff they serve at the church."

He was right. It was a perfectly chilled French Colombard. The evening was taking a turn for the better, one cool sip at a time. Olympia sniffed and then tasted the contents of the glass and made a good show of savoring its elegance. He was right; this was good wine.

"Before I forget, here's the ice cream." Olympia handed Jack a plastic grocery bag, "I got French vanilla and mango sorbet. They go well together."

"An evening of French delights?" said her host.

Olympia ignored him and asked Janney if she could help in the kitchen.

Janney stuck her head through the half-door leading to the space below. "It's called a galley, and actually, I'm done. I just need another drink. Come on down and see the place, and I'll give you the five-second tour. Watch your head."

Olympia ducked and stepped down into the tiny galley. "How did you get supper in the oven so fast?"

"I unwrapped the box. The tough part was turning on the oven." They both laughed. Janney was pouring a lot of gin into a tall glass. "Want a G and T?"

Olympia shook her head and held up her almost full glass. "No, thanks," This is simply elegant. I wouldn't switch for anything."

"I like a minister who knows how to drink. Let me top you up." Janney took careful aim but sloshed a bit over the top as the microwave dinged, announcing their dinner. "Damn, that was quick. Well, it can stay there and keep itself warm while we finish our drinks. C'mon, let's see who the old man's up to. I gotta watch that boy."

Janney turned and moved up the polished steps and led the way back onto the party deck. Jack, with a drink in one hand and a tortilla chip in the other, introduced Olympia to his next-boat neighbor.

She smiled politely through the trite pleasantries, knowing she would not possibly remember the names. As soon as she graciously could, she turned back to join Janney, who was glassy eyed and listing seriously to port on one of the deck benches.

Jack shook his head and steered Olympia to a deck chair on the starboard side of the craft. "She does that, switches off like a light. She's been an alcoholic for years. She'll come to in an hour or so and want something to eat and then have another drink. I guess I'm used to it by now. I take care of her, she takes care of me. It's a trade-off."

Olympia put down her glass. "I think I should leave, Jack. When she does wake up, she'll be mortified."

"I only wish she would be, then maybe she'd stop. She just makes a sloppy joke of it and then has another drink. Our friends understand. Welcome to the island, Olympia. But please stay and have supper with me."

This time the eyebrow didn't go up, and there were no overtones. Jack handed Olympia her glass. "I can open a take-out box as well as the next guy. We'll be right here when she wakes up, then I'll feed her and put her to bed. It's a lonely life, Olympia, and I wouldn't mind some company. There's nobody to talk to after six in the evening." He checked his watch. "I guess she started early, it's just after five-thirty."

"Has she ever gone to AA?"

Jack paused and looked straight at Olympia. "She won't go. I tried. Says she doesn't need it. As I said, it's a trade-off, and besides that, I love her. We manage."

Olympia accepted the glass but set it on the table.

"OK," she said, "but just for dinner. My sermon still needs writing. "

Olympia looked at the unhappy man standing in front of her, "Jack, are you sure there isn't something I can do?"

Jack lowered his voice and looked away from Olympia. "Well, now that you asked, I guess I could use a minister right now."

Nine

Eudora West stood just inside the open door. She had a lace-edged handkerchief in her light brown hand.

"Why, William Bateson, what a nice surprise, I wasn't expecting you. What brings you here at this time of day?

"I was driving through the neighborhood and thought I'd check on my favorite church lady. I'm heading into town and wondered if you needed anything."

"How very kind. I'm all set for now, but how about a cup of tea before you go?"

William looked pleasantly surprised. "Why, how did you know what I really wanted was a cup of tea? Now that we both know what I'm up to, why don't you let me make it? That is, unless you'd rather have something stronger. Isn't it about that time?" William gave a broad wink and raised an imaginary glass.

"Tea will be fine, Mr. Bateson, especially when I have somebody so nice to share it with."

"Then you stay here on the sofa and let me attend to the women's work."

Eudora giggled and waved him off toward the kitchen. With a contented sigh, she settled back on the sofa. From where she sat, she couldn't see William Bateson methodically opening drawers and cupboards and looking at the underside of the sink. While he was making the noises of making their tea, he ran a practiced hand along the bit of wall under the window over the sink and scribbled a few notes on a scrap of paper. He stuffed the paper into his trousers pocket and called out to Eudora.

"I'll need something without caffeine. Aha, just the thing, peppermint tea, that'll be perfect. Good for the stomach at this end of the day."

Eudora called back from the next room. "What did you say, dear? I can't hear you when the water's running."

William smiled and poured their tea, but before he returned to the living room, he slipped a tiny camera out of his breast pocket and snapped several pictures of the vintage 1940s kitchen with its porcelain sink, worn wooden counters and painted cupboards.

"Did you just blow a light bulb? I thought I saw a flash."

William quickly stuffed the camera back in his jacket and carried the tea tray into the living room.

"No, but I'll check around before I leave. It was probably a reflection off a passing car. Let's have our tea first. Do you want anything else in yours, a little honey maybe? I found some and put it on the tray."

"Just a little milk." Eudora was politely covering a yawn.

"Already in there," said William. "I haven't forgotten how you like your tea, but I thought you might like to try it with some honey. Very soothing on the tummy."

"Why, Mr. Bateson, I must say you certainly know how to be nice to a lady".

"My dear Mrs. West, you are very easy to be nice to."

He picked up his own teacup and leaned back in the creaky wicker chair across from Eudora. "The last time I was here you started to tell me about the house and how you came to own it. You said it was your mother's. I like house stories. Didn't you say you were one of the first African American families to have a house on the Island?"

Eudora stirred her tea, set the teaspoon in her saucer and settled into a story she loved to tell. "We were indeed. They used to call us colored folks back then. It was hard for an African American family to buy property here, but my father got this house from a white man he worked for. The old man died and left it to him. Nobody in his family wanted it, and my father had been very good to him when he got old." She sat up straighter and adjusted the sofa cushions around her. She had come to the part of the story she most loved to tell and liked to take her time.

"My mother first started coming to the Vineyard in the summer after she graduated from college. She was one of the first black women ever to attend college, you know. She loved it here so much that when she met my father, they decided to stay here year round. Mother was a teacher, and my father was a carpenter." She gestured to the stairway beyond the door. "I was born right up those stairs, but I won't tell you how long ago. And mother died in the same room right there in her own bed with me sitting right beside her."

Eudora's eyes misted with the memory, and a solicitous William Bateson reached over, patted her hand and held out a freshly ironed white handkerchief.

She shook her head and waved him away. "Still gets to me. So many memories. Some days I can forget what I had for lunch or who I talked to on the phone, but this story is in my bones."

Bateson nodded sympathetically. "When did you say the original part of the house was built?"

"Late1800s. I've got the exact date in my papers upstairs in my office—well, actually in the spare bedroom I use as an office." Eudora leaned back into the cushions and crossed her feet. "The original house was this room, the dining room and the kitchen downstairs, and two bedrooms upstairs. 'Course, we added on to it since then, but we are sitting in the same room where my father proposed to my mother."

She put down her tea cup and looked wistfully around the room.

"And where they were eventually married," added William.

She nodded.

"But since your husband died, you say the house is becoming a burden."

"Maybe it is." She fingered one of the buttons on her sweater. "But where would I go? I've lived here all my life and besides," Dory lifted her chin. "I talk about moving, but in the end, I'll probably be carried out of here just like my mother." She dabbed at her eyes again and covered another yawn with her handkerchief. She was beginning to nod off.

William looked down at his watch and began to collect the teacups.

"Goodness gracious me, look at the time. It's going to be a long time before you leave here, Miss Eudora." He paused, tray in hand. "But if you think the house is getting too big for you and the upkeep is getting too much, and you ever think about moving into something smaller, I'm the one who can help you. It's always better to trust someone you know, right?"

He looked down at the drowsy woman seated in front of him, and when she was almost asleep, he turned and went into the kitchen. He took his time as he rinsed off the cups and spoons and set them upside down on the wooden drain to dry. When he returned, Dory's head had fallen forward, and she was breathing slowly and evenly. She stirred as he entered the room.

"Oh, dear, I guess we chatted past my nap-time. I'm sorry, it's just …" She was already drifting back off.

"My fault entirely, I didn't keep track of the time. Do you mind if I use the bathroom before I leave? I know where it is. You just stay where you are. I can let myself out. Shall I tuck your afghan around you?"

She nodded again, her eyes closing.

He pulled the knitted blanket over her lap and then went back into the kitchen where he splashed water in the sink and flushed the toilet. When he returned she was breathing slowly and evenly and made no response when he asked if she knew what time it was. She never heard him go back to the kitchen, stuff a dish cloth into the drain and turn on the water. With that done, he quietly walked past her and let himself out the front door. He made no sound at all as he walked across the old wooden porch and down the steps to his car. The sentimental old woman would be out for at least an hour, and that was all the time that was necessary.

Ten

Sitting in a blue and white striped canvas chair on the deck of the *Janney-Lee*, Olympia could hear Jack Winters rummaging around in the galley. Earlier, he'd covered his wife with a light blanket, and she was still out when he returned carrying two plates of something that smelled wonderful. He had utensils and napkins tucked into his shirt pocket and a second bottle of the French Colombard wedged under his arm.

He set the blue and white dishes on the table and then, with a courtly flourish, arranged the knives and forks and pulled the plastic salt and pepper containers out of his back pocket. They had snap-on covers to keep out the damp. Olympia remembered having a set like them when she was little. Her mother won them at a Tupperware party. The pop of a wine cork brought her back to the present.

She shook her head and held up her hand. "Thanks, Jack, no more for me. Even though it's not very far, I'm driving, and I'm a minister. Wouldn't do if I couldn't pass a breathalyzer test on my second day here, now would it? So thank you, but no."

The tone in her voice said she meant it, and Jack put down the bottle. He didn't even pour a glass for himself.

Olympia looked over at Janney and lowered her voice, "What is it you wanted to talk about?"

"Not now. Let's have our dinner first, and then we can take a little walk along the harbor. I really don't want to take a chance on her hearing this. She'll know soon enough."

The man sitting across from her was clearly worried about something, and by the look of him, it was serious. Originally, Olympia thought he was being flirty, but all of that changed the instant Janney passed out. Maybe she was his social shield. She had known other couples like that. The guy flirts like crazy, making passes and innuendoes all over the place as long as his wife is around, but when she goes out of the room, it all stops. She'd had second thoughts about staying on for dinner back in the parking lot, but maybe it wasn't a mistake after all.

The two swayed with the movement of the vessel and talked easily about the church and the weather and the clever engineering of pleasure boats as they worked their way through their meal. She decided Jack winters was a personable man, after all, but he was also a very troubled one and wondered what in the world it was that he wanted to tell her.

Olympia set her knife and fork side by side on the plate and looked at the man sitting across from her. "I don't want to rush you, Jack, but maybe we could go for that walk now?"

Jack looked over at his sleeping wife. A flicker of pain creased his forehead, "She's good for another half hour, and what I have to say isn't going to take long. I'll clean up after you go."

He held out his hand to Olympia, and she stepped off the boat onto the sidewalk. The tide had been coming in since she'd gotten there, and the angle was considerably steeper. They walked for a while without speaking. As she looked at the boats nudging against the dock and listened to the sounds of gulls begging for scraps and then squabbling over who got the biggest, Olympia was carefully leaving space and time for the man to speak when he was ready. This place was so different from anything she had ever experienced, and she couldn't wait to show it all to Frederick. If there wasn't a drunken woman asleep on a million dollar pleasure cruiser, and the husband of that woman wasn't about to tell her something he needed to say in secret, it might be a perfect summer evening on a storybook island off the south coast of Massachusetts. Only it wasn't, and she knew it.

She was about to ask herself how she got herself into this when Jack stopped at one of the public benches facing the water and invited her to sit down beside him. She sat, folded her hands in her lap, and waited for Jack to speak.

"Thank you, Olympia, or should I be calling you Reverend Olympia?"

"Olympia is fine. What is it you want to tell me?"

Jack looked out into the harbor. "I got a bad biopsy report this morning. I have colon cancer. Janney doesn't know."

Olympia blinked and steadied her voice. "How bad, Jack?"

"Stage three, maybe worse. They'll know for sure when they go in and have a look. The doctor said best case scenario is surgery, a bag and a chemo for a while. Then if that works, maybe they can reverse it. Worst case … well, I guess I don't have to say it."

Jack turned and looked directly at Olympia. The fear and resignation were evident in his eyes.

"When is it scheduled?"

"They call it a procedure these days." He half laughed, half choked. "A life-and-death fucking procedure!" He put his hand over his mouth and looked away. "I'm sorry, Olympia, that was rude."

"I've heard worse. How can I help?"

"I don't know," he said, "it's all so new. I go next week, Monday morning. They've already set it up. I'm going into the Dana Farber Cancer Center in Boston." He paused. "It feels good to be able to tell someone."

"You need to tell Janney."

"I know, Olympia, but I haven't a clue where to begin."

Olympia turned and placed her hand on his shoulder. "You've begun by telling me, Jack. It's not going to be easy, but now you aren't alone. You need to get back to your wife, but don't say anything tonight while she's still … not herself. Why don't you come and see me in the church office tomorrow morning? I can be there by nine-thirty."

"OK if I bring my coffee?" Jack was trying to sound casual."

"As long as you bring one for me, black, please, with lots of caffeine."

Jack looked down at his watch. "I think she might be surfacing. I should go."

"I can find my way back to the car, Jack. Thank you for supper."

Olympia stood and left the man standing alone on the sidewalk with his head bowed and his arms crossed in front of him. If he was correct in his calculations, Janney was due to wake up any minute. What then? When she drove past the Janney Lee on her way home, the sky was beginning to go fuchsia and gold over the water … and Jack Winter was still standing on the sidewalk.

Eleven

The long light of the June evening made it easy for her to find her way back to her cottage. The main roads were relatively free of tourist traffic, and in less than fifteen minutes she was almost home. The car clock said quarter to nine. There would still be time to pay some attention to the cats and get started on her sermon. But all of that evaporated when she turned onto her street and saw the fire truck parked outside the house.

She pulled over two houses away, exploded out of the car and raced across the street, thinking only of the cats, when she realized that the firefighters were outside Dory's house. They were positioning a hose that was coming out of her cellar window and gushing water into the street.

"What happened? Where's Mrs. West?" Olympia was almost shouting at the man who was trying to position the hose, "Is she hurt? What in God's name has happened?"

"She's pretty shook up, but she's OK. You know her?" The man guiding the hose was dressed in full fire gear.

"She's my landlady, I'm Olympia Brown. I'm staying in the guest house. Where is she?" He looked over at her house and pointed a muddy finger.

"She left the water running and took a nap. We've seen it before. They get old and start forgetting things. She flooded the first floor. Most of it went down to the basement. That's what we're pumping out now. Gonna be one hell of a mess, though. Gonna smell real bad in a few days, too. I hope she's got insurance."

Olympia thanked him and ran into the house, where she found Dory sitting on the sofa looking dazed. She had bright blue rubber boots on her feet, and from where Olympia stood she could see William Bateson in the kitchen, pushing water out of the back door with a large broom. The rugs had been pulled up, and the wide planks of the floor were already starting to buckle.

"Dory, what happened?"

"I don't know, Olympia. William dropped in this afternoon, and we had tea. He says I did the dishes, but I don't remember doing them. I thought he said he was going to take care of them. I was tired. Oh, dear, it's all a blur." Dory was twisting one of her handkerchiefs. It was pink with a crocheted lace edge and matched her sweater.

"Take your time." Olympia was trying to make sense of what she was hearing. "You had tea with Mr. Bateson, and then he left, and you went and washed out the cups."

"No. We had tea, and then I started getting sleepy, and I think he did the dishes. I can't remember, but I did go to sleep, and when I woke up there was water everywhere. I almost fell going into the kitchen to shut off the faucet. There was a dishcloth stuck in the drain. How could I have done such a stupid thing?"

Olympia put one arm lightly around Dory's slender shoulders and patted her trembling hands. "I'm going to call Julia Scott-Norton and Leigh Mayhew. You can't stay here tonight. We'll get you dry and settled, and then we'll deal with the water, the insurance people and anything else that needs to be done tomorrow."

Olympia leaned closer and kissed her cheek. "Let me go and talk to William. I'm sure he'll be willing to help us. By the way, when did he get here?"

Dory didn't answer her but kept repeating, "I just don't know how this happened."

"It could happen to anyone. I left the bathwater running once. I flooded the kitchen downstairs. I felt awful, but it was an accident, and so is this. We'll get it fixed." Olympia was trying her best to sound reassuring.

She was moving through the chaos of wet rugs, stacked furniture and curling magazines toward the kitchen where she could see William Bateson. He was in his shirtsleeves, still pushing at the pools of water.

"Poor thing," he semi-whispered over his shoulder, "fell asleep and left the water running. I knew I should have done those dishes for her. We had tea together just before it happened. I offered, but you know how independent she is. Wouldn't hear of it, and now this." He sloshed some more water through the kitchen door into the back hall where it gurgled down the stairs into the cellar.

Olympia put her hands on her hips and surveyed the situation. "She can't stay here tonight. I have a church directory next door. She's probably got one, too, but I don't want to ask her for anything at the moment. Will you stay here until I get back?"

He stopped sweeping and leaned on his push-broom "Of course I will. I'll do anything I can. I'm very fond of her, but between you and me, I don't think it's safe for her to live alone much longer. The next time it could be worse."

Olympia nodded in uneasy agreement and turned back toward the living room. "I'll be right back. Good thing you came by. That was a lucky coincidence. Did you just happen to be in the neighborhood?"

"I don't live far away, so I kind of keep an eye on her. I like older people. My grandmother raised me, so I'm comfortable being with them. Lucky for her I did come by. I drive around these neighborhoods for my business. When she woke up and found the water, she called the fire department. I heard the sirens and followed the sound. Poor thing was completely disoriented. She's better now."

"I'll be right back," Olympia called over her shoulder.

"And I'll be right here," came the answer.

After Olympia walked out of the house and closed the door, William Bateson counted to ten, put down his push-broom and walked back to the living room where Dory was still sitting twisting her handkerchief and shaking her head. She turned toward him as he entered the room.

"What am I going to do? It's all so overwhelming." She pressed her handkerchief against her lips.

He went over and sat down beside her and started to pull the afghan back over her legs, but she gestured him away with an impatient wave of her free hand.

"Thank you, dear, but I'm not cold. My house is a wreck, and I don't know how this all happened, and I don't know where I'm going to sleep tonight, but I don't need a blanket right now. It would help if you could manage to find a light and turn it on. The water is bad enough. I don't want to sit in a wet house that is dark, as well." Her eyes were bright and clear.

"They shut off the power because of the flood," said William. "Have you got a flashlight or something, maybe a couple of candles?" He stood up again, looking at the chaos around him.

"I keep an emergency battery light under the sink and another one in my bedroom. The one under the sink is probably wet, but the one in my bedroom should be OK, I just tested it. I always keep extra batteries. You never know when you are going to lose power here, and I'm too old to wander around in the dark."

"Good thinking, Mrs. West." Bateson pushed himself up off the low-slung sofa and started toward the hallway. "I'll go upstairs and get it. Which one is your bedroom?"

"Mine is the room on the left at the top of the stairs. The lamp is right beside the bed on the night table. The bathroom's straight ahead, if you need it. The one down here is a total mess."

Bateson paused on the landing and called out, "I see it."

Once he was inside Dory's bedroom, he took his time picking up the lamp and turning a switch to see if it worked. As he did so, a pale bluish light flooded the room. In that light William found what he expected to find in an old lady's bedroom: family pictures on a white painted dresser of indeterminate vintage, an old quilt folded and placed at a slight angle over the foot of the bed. On the wicker night stand beside the bed there was a box of tissues, a bottle of aspirin and a half-full glass of water. Beside that was a large print mystery novel by Island author Cynthia Riggs. It was marked with a lace bookmark, ready for that evening's chapter. The room was meticulously neat and smelled faintly of lavender and cedar.

He walked out of the bedroom, eased open the door across the landing and stepped inside. He did a quick inventory, mentally assessing the shape and condition of the space and cataloging the furnishings in what he assumed was Dory's guest room. In the fading light he could see a day bed against the far wall, another painted chest and an old wooden writing desk set squarely in front of the dormered window, presumably to take advantage of the natural light. On top of the desk he could see an orderly arrangement of file folders and papers.

She must use this as her office.

He stepped back out of the room and into the bathroom where he flushed the toilet, then waited a moment or two before coming back downstairs with the emergency lamp.

"That's better," he said setting the black plastic lantern on the coffee table in front of Dory. "Not much better, mind you, but at least it's something. Maybe a candle would ..."

"No candles please, dear, they make me nervous, even with you here and me wide awake. I never use them anymore. Too easy to forget."

"Yes indeed, Eudora. You can never be too careful. You know, maybe when I come back tomorrow, it might be time to ..."

But he never finished the sentence, because Olympia simultaneously knocked and burst through the front door. She was breathing heavily and patting her chest.

"I'm back! I ran all the way—all twenty five feet and six inches between my front door and yours. I've still got electricity, by the way. How are you holding up, Dory? Julia Scott-Norton is on her way. She would like you to stay with her until we sort things with the fire department and the insurance company. You've been to Julia's house. I was there myself today." *Was it only four hours ago?* "She must have twenty bedrooms, well, OK, maybe five or six. But she's got loads of room. What do you think?"

"That would be wonderful, I ..." Dory's chin began to quiver, and the tears she had been fighting back all evening rolled down her cheeks and fell unchecked onto the printed flowers on her blouse.

Olympia sat down beside her and looked up at William Bateson. She nodded toward the kitchen in a silent request that he leave them alone. Did she see a flicker of annoyance in his eyes? No, if it was anything, surely it was concern for Dory.

She could hear the sound of the sump pump sucking the water out of the basement window. It was an ugly sound. Olympia spoke softly to the woman sitting beside her.

"Would you like me to gather up a few things to take with you for the night? You know, a nightie and a robe and maybe your toothbrush. How about your medicines? We can always come back and get more tomorrow."

Dory hesitated only a moment. "Would you mind? If you could get my nightie from under the pillow, the robe is on the back of the door. I keep my pills in my purse. That way, I always know where they are." She looked toward the kitchen and lowered her voice to a whisper that William could not possibly hear. "My small clothes are in the top drawer of the dresser, one of each please, the light blue ones. My bedroom is the one on the left at the top of the stairs. And my toothbrush, please—it's in a glass on the bathroom sink."

When he heard footsteps on the staircase, Bateson returned to the living room and stood just inside the doorway.

"Everything OK in here?"

"Olympia is upstairs gathering up a few things for me to take tonight. I guess I'm going to Julia Scott-Norton's."

"I was here when Olympia suggested it, don't you remember?"

"I ..."

Once again, the front door opened, and Julia Scott-Norton, in all of her blessed efficiency, strode into the room as Olympia returned with Dory's night clothes, small things, and toothbrush, discreetly folded into a towel. On top of it all was the unfinished mystery novel.

Julia took one look at the collection in Olympia's hands and said, "I have a plastic grocery sack in my purse. I always keep one or two with me. Never know when you'll need them."

Julia turned to hand the plastic bag to Olympia and spotted William Bateson standing across the room. "Good heavens, how did you get here so fast?"

Olympia slipped Dory's things into the plastic bag as she responded to Julia. "He was in the neighborhood when he heard the sirens, and a good thing it was, too. He followed the sound and found Dory ankle deep in water."

Dory lifted her legs and pointed to the rubber boots on her feet. "First thing he did was put these things on my feet. I don't know what I would have done if my feet got wet."

Julia looked around at the soggy mess in the room. "Olympia told me you called 911. You knew what to do. Anyone would be overwhelmed to find their house flooded. Come on, Dory, I'm taking you home with me. We'll deal with all of this tomorrow. Where's your cane, dear?"

"On the doorknob, but I only use it when I go out."

Julia winked at Olympia and then turned to William Bateson.

"I can't thank you enough. You just stepped in and took over, but I don't think there is anything more any of us can do today. The firemen are packing up, and Olympia and I will be able to give or take down any information that might be necessary."

She paused and smiled, "So it looks like you're off duty, Mr. Bateson. You are going to need a well-deserved rest after all this." There was no mistaking the firm note of dismissal under Julia's enthusiastic display of appreciation.

William retrieved his briefcase from beside the staircase and turned to Dory. "Anything I can do, my dear lady, you just call me. You have my card in your purse, and you know my numbers." He stood and inclined his head toward Julia and Olympia, "Thank you, ladies. I'm not going to worry. I know she's in good hands."

When they heard the sound of his car driving off, Julia called Olympia out into the kitchen, saying she just wanted to have one last look around before they left. The wet wood smell was curiously pleasant, but Olympia thought it best not to say so at the moment. *Could be a wee bit tactless just now.*

Julia lowered her voice so Dory couldn't hear. "Maybe she is starting to lose it. Up until today I wouldn't have said so, but after this, I'm not so sure. On the other hand, something like this would upset Mother Theresa. We'll just wait and see how she is over the next few days. I'll call her daughter tomorrow. Nothing is going to change between now and the morning, and in the meanwhile I'll see what Dory can tell me when it's quiet and she's had a chance to calm down. Do you mind staying after we leave and opening a few windows and then locking the place?"

Twelve

As Olympia listened to the sound of them driving off, she walked around the sodden house, telling herself that it really could have happened to anybody. Tomorrow Julia or somebody would call the insurance people and the flooded house experts, whoever or whatever they might be, and get things rolling. She shook her head in dismay. The floorboards creaked under her feet, and little pools of water formed around her sandals as she picked her way through the mess. She could hear water dripping. *Probably down in the basement, but there's no way in hell I'm going down to look.* Suddenly the whole thing felt creepy.

By now the firemen had taken away the pump, and all was quiet except for the creaks and groans of an old house trying to shake itself dry and not succeeding. Olympia was just about to leave when she noticed a file folder lying on the staircase. Seeing it there made her think that she should probably go up those stairs and open a few windows and get some more fresh air in the place. She stepped over the folder and started up the creaky stairs, holding Dory's emergency camping lantern in front of her. When she was almost to the top, she slipped on something and fell forward, slamming the lantern on the floor in front of her and leaving her in total darkness. *Jesus! I need this like I need a hole in the head.*

As her eyes adjusted to the darkness, she felt around on the stair tread to find out what it was she'd stepped on and found a pencil. *Good thing it was me that stepped on it and not Dory. That could be really dangerous for someone as old as she is.* In the light cast by the street lamp outside, she felt her way back into Dory's bedroom and pushed up the two windows as high as they would go. Having gathered some confidence, she made her way into the bathroom and managed to get the tiny window over an old-fashioned claw foot tub open and up by about an inch. Now all that remained was the guest room. Her eyes were fully adjusted to the dark by now. Aided by the light from a full moon on the other side of the house, she could see a desk under the single window and what was probably a bed against a far wall. She slipped her feet across the painted boards and felt something soft brush against her ankle. Olympia jumped, screamed, and kicked all at the same and then looked down to see that her attacker was a scatter rug.

"This is just not my night," Olympia spoke aloud into the darkness as she continued feeling her way across the room to open the window over the writing desk. The smooth surface of the desk top reflected the moonlight into the orderly room, making it easier to see. There was a plastic container with several manila folders tucked into it. It was too dark to read them, but thinking that this might be information that Dory could need tomorrow, she tucked the container under her arm and took one last look around. There was no clutter to be seen anywhere. Even the work area on her desk was empty except for a tiny pot of pencils and pens.

She turned and went out of the room and inched her way down the stairs to the living room. The light of moon and street lamp did not carry far enough around corners of the stairwell to light the entire way, but once back in the living room, she could see her way safely to the door. Before she left she returned to the stairs and picked up the orphan folder and added it to the others under her arm.

After she had locked and tested all the doors, she tucked the key under the overturned flower pot beside the door. With that accomplished, she made her way through the sodden grass back to her own little cottage. Perhaps with an uninterrupted hour or two, she would wind down with a glass of wine and consider her sermon. But as she pushed open her front door, she clapped her hand to her mouth. *Frederick! I was supposed to have called him hours ago. Oh, crap!*

She flipped on the light and put the plastic box of folders on the table. By some miracle both the electricity and the phone in her side of the house were still working. The cats were both dancing around and squawking for food, but they could wait. She sat down, lifted the receiver and tapped in her Brookfield number. Olympia found herself weak with gratitude and longing when she heard a very welcome voice say, "Frederick Watkins here."

"Oh, Frederick, it's me, Olympia."

"I know who it is, Dearie, I'd know that New England twang anywhere. I'm glad you called. I have some important news for you. I had no idea how to reach you. I left a message at the church, but I guess nobody told you. By the way, I miss you fiercely, and I love you. Just thought I'd get that out before you could change the subject. And if you want, I'll bring your phone down when I come over there, which could be tomorrow morning if you so desire."

"Frederick?"

"Oh, dear, something's wrong isn't it? I can hear it in your voice, and you've been gone a little over twenty-four hours. What in the bloody hell have you managed to get yourself embroiled in this time?"

"Nothing bad, Frederick, at least I don't think so. At the moment it's just messy."

"Olympia, dearest, I am not understanding you."

"OK, short form: my landlady fell asleep with the water running and flooded her house. My place is OK. We've packed her off with a church member for safe keeping. I'm using her extension. Thank heaven it still works. So you see, it's not really a problem, it's just an inconvenience of proximity. Now, what's your news?"

"I think you'd better be sitting down. Your daughter called when we were both out yesterday. She left a number. She wants to meet you."

"Oh, my God, let me go get something I can write with."

Olympia got up to find a pencil and was surprised to find her hands shaking and her knees wobbling. This was too wonderful for comprehension, and it was also completely overwhelming. A lifetime of waiting, and now what? Of course she would call her daughter, but not until morning. It was too late, and she was an emotional train wreck.

When she finally located the stub of a pencil in the kitchen, she wrote down the number and spent the next few minutes trying to catch Frederick up on all that had happened since they had parted company. He, in turn, filled her in on his various projects, but Olympia wasn't hearing a word. She made polite noises at seemingly appropriate intervals, but in reality she was beyond thinking and finally admitted it. Frederick, bless him, really meant it when he offered to come down on the first boat out the next day. So he could be with her when she called her daughter, was the reason he gave, but Olympia declined. Much as she loved him (*yes, dammit, loved him*), she simply could not add him to everything else that was going on around her. She tried to explain it, and Frederick, bless him again, said he understood. She would, she promised, call him right after she talked with Laura, but right now, she needed a glass of wine and an hour of utter and complete silence.

When she finally finished her wine, Olympia stood by the window for a moment of reflective peace and quiet. Despite the chaos of the day, her heart rate had returned to normal, and she was actually enjoying the sounds of the night and watching the moon shadows flittering on the grass between her cottage and the main house. It was such a clear night. She looked up at the sky and realized that she could see so many more stars here than she could in Brookfield, and she looked forward to sharing this with Frederick. Everything had happened so fast. Their original plan had been to spend the summer working on the house in Brookfield to see if living together might be a viable option for their combined futures. Now even that was on hold.

The moon shadows on the lawn and the side of the house were dreamlike, and she realized she was finally getting sleepy. From where she stood, she could just see the corner of Dory's house and the upstairs guest room window. Olympia did a double take. *Did I just see something move in there?* Was that a person in the window, or was it the cast shadow of a tree branch across the glass?

She was so tired that her eyes must be playing tricks on her. She remembered being frightened out of her wits by tree shadows on her bedroom wall when she was little. On a windy night with a full moon rising, the angular skeletal shadows turned into vampires and monsters crawling across the walls and the ceiling, slowly creeping down to get her. She shook off the memory. She told herself that was then and this is now, and what you see is the shadow of a tree branch. *Time to go to bed, Olympia. You're hallucinating.*

As she was drifting off to sleep, just before the final descent, she heard the sound of a car starting and wondered who in the neighborhood would be going out at this hour of the night. Then she slept.

Thirteen

December 1, 1860

To my consummate joy I have discovered the Widener Library at Harvard College. Every day that weather and walking conditions permit, I ensconce myself at one of the great long polished oak tables and read until my eyes grow weary and darkness begins to fall. I will thus continue for as long as I can, until even the most bulky of winter cloaks and shawls no longer disguise my condition. I am sadly amused that a woman's pregnancy is delicately referred to as her 'confinement'. Is it because well-bred women in the so-called family way are expected to stay hidden from view? It must be, because for a woman to be obviously pregnant means she has just as obviously engaged in sexual intercourse, and we aren't supposed to admit to that. I find it all to be distressingly hypocritical, and despite the protestations of my darling aunt, I refused to stay hidden.

Once she knew that I planned to keep the baby, she begged me to stay on with her in Cambridge saying she would love to have a child in the house. But after swearing on her well-worn family Bible that I...no, we would visit often, she understood that this was something I had chosen to do myself. And so we wait. With no house and garden chores to occupy my time, I have only my reading, and knitting for my coming child, to pass the shortening days. Alas, the nights are a different matter. In the dark, with no one as witness, I put my hands on my growing belly and think of the man that both honor and decency decree...that I must never see again.

More anon, LFW

~

Olympia surprised herself by sleeping until almost seven the next morning, but upon waking, her first thought was of her daughter. This morning, within the hour, she would speak to the child, now a woman ... the child she held only once, minutes after she was born, before she was taken away. The child she had ached to see and touch every single day that had passed since that time, and now she was a total mess. Maybe she should have allowed Frederick to come. *No, I need to do this myself.*

She thought back to the day only weeks ago when she had told him about her daughter and what it was like trying to find her. She didn't know what to expect, but after hearing the story he simply put his arms around her and said how wonderful it was and was there any way he could help. No shock, no condemnation, only tenderness and caring for her pain and now her thread of hope. *Yes, this one was different.* Her two sons, Malcolm and Randall, had been more reserved in their responses to the news of their half-sister, but after a few cautious questions, they said they were glad they knew, and maybe one day they might like to meet her, and let it go at that. All in all it had been better than she feared and less than she'd hoped for.

She got up, showered and dressed but decided against having any coffee; she was already totally wired. After feeding the cats she went and stood by the window and looked over at Dory's house. It appeared unchanged from the night before. *Maybe I should go over and check it.* She was stalling, putting off for a last few minutes what she most wanted and most feared.

Just do it, Olympia, nothing can be worse than what you've been through all these years. Oh, yes it can!

She picked up the piece of paper with her daughter's number on it and reached for the phone. Then she had to sit down because her legs suddenly seemed to have taken on a life of their own. She tried squeezing her eyes shut but realized she couldn't see the dial pad. Finally, she took a deep breath and with a trembling finger tapped in the number. Then she almost hung up when she heard the phone, wherever it was, start ringing. Three rings, four rings. If she didn't pick up, Olympia would not leave a message. *Not this time.* She started to replace the receiver when she heard a sleepy voice.

"M-m-hello?"

"Laura? Laura Wilstrom?"

"This is Laura."

"Laura, this is Olympia Brown. I'm your birth mother."

"I wondered if you'd call." The words were measured and cool.

Olympia could not control her voice or her shaking hands or the tears that ran out of her eyes and dripped off her chin. "Thank God I've found you," was all she could get out before her emotions took over completely. When she regained some small measure of control, she added, "You said in your message you were willing to meet me. You have no idea how long I have prayed for this to happen. Tell me when and where, and I'll be there."

"Where are you now?"

"I'm on Martha's Vineyard."

"Well, that's not too hard to take. I guess you're doing pretty well."

"I don't live here year-round, Laura. I'm a minister, and I took a summer position in a community church here. I can get away. It might just take me a little longer because of the ferry and all."

"You married?" asked her daughter.

"No, not any more. All of that was a long time ago."

"Me either. I'm living in Somerville. We could meet somewhere in between."

"I could come there," said Olympia.

"I'd rather you didn't."

The shaking started again. Olympia clenched her fists. "The weather is supposed to be pretty good for the next few days. We could meet in Boston, in the Public Garden. We could walk or sit on a bench and talk or even go for a coffee or something, if you wanted."

"That'll work. When do you think?"

Olympia wanted to scream, "I can be on the next ferry, or I can try walking on water, if you want me to," but she realized that neither was practical or possible. "Would next Monday be good for you? If it rains, we can find a restaurant or a church to go into. We could meet near the swan boats."

"Monday would work. Eleven o'clock. I can take a personal day."

A personal day. Of course, she's is a grown woman now. She has a job, and she's going to have a baby, I'm going to be a grandmother, and I only just found out my daughter's name and what she looks like.

"Eleven is perfect. By the swan boats? I'll be carrying a teddy bear."

"A teddy bear?"

"For the baby."

"Oh, OK."

"Laura, there's so much to say, and I don't know how to say it or where to begin. The most important thing for you to know right now is that I love you and I've always loved you. Not a day has passed since I gave birth to you that I haven't wondered where you were and how you were doing."

"So why did you wait so long?" Her voice was flat.

"I wanted to, but the people in the Department of Records told me it was best not to contact you. They said that it could make things difficult for you and your adoptive parents."

"My parents."

"Can we begin this conversation on Monday, Laura?"

"That's probably a good idea." There was a long silence before she spoke again. "I'm glad you called me. I wasn't sure if you would."

"And I wasn't sure what I'd say when I did. I guess we managed."

"We managed. I guess I'll see you on Monday."

When Olympia hung up the phone, the only thing she could think of to do was to take off her clothes and go back into the shower. When she emerged, bright pink from the hot water and her eyes puffy from crying, she splashed cold water on her face, rubbed her swollen eyes with ice, and set off for the church. She had a nine-thirty appointment, and it was nine-fifteen. *Shift gears, Olympia. You're a minister, and you've got a job to do.*

At nine-thirty exactly Jack Winters walked through the door of the church office.

True to his promise of the night before, he was carrying two steaming containers of coffee from a local restaurant and a white paper bakery sack. Given the start to her morning, Olympia had not had much of a breakfast and was grateful for his thoughtfulness. He set the paper bag on the edge of the desk between them and handed Olympia one of the containers.

"Basic black, high test for the minister-lady," he paused dramatically, "and her choice of sugar-free, fat-free oat bran muffins with free range, organic, corn fed raisins, or without."

Olympia chuckled, popped back the drinking tab on the top of the coffee and eyed the package containing the muffins. "Is that to counteract the inherent dangers of caffeine? Or are you determined make me healthy in spite of myself? I have a priest friend who sometimes thinks he's my personal trainer and drags me off for brisk, health-giving walks whenever he can." She was trying to keep the conversation light, at least for now.

"Despite the healthy ingredients, these are really pretty good. Janney and I get them by the dozen and freeze them. We thaw out two at a time for breakfast when we stay on the boat. It's probably one of the few healthy things we do." He bit his lip and looked down at the floor. "I guess it didn't work."

"Sit down, Jack. Let's have our coffee and give me one of those muffins you're so enthusiastic about. I'll have the one with the raisins, and when we're finished we can talk more about what you told me last night. I'm not in any hurry. I got a good night's sleep despite all the excitement last night. Once we got Dory West over to the Scott-Norton's and settled in, it was clear sailing. *Well, not by a long-shot, if I were to be honest, but we are talking about your problems, not mine, Mr. Winters.* I don't have to be home until this afternoon, when the insurance adjusters come to meet with Mrs. West."

The look on his face said that he had no idea what Olympia was talking about. So she filled him in on the details of what had happened, how it happened, who was there, and her own dismay at seeing Dory so upset.

"William Bateson, huh? Little Willie on the spot, always there when you need him whether you think so or not. I tell you, Olympia, I don't like that guy."

Olympia started to speak, but Jack Winters continued, warming to his rant, "Oh, I know, he's fussy and he sucks up to the old ladies … oops, 'scuse me, Rev, but I think there is something going on underneath that swishy appearance of his. Maybe it's a guy thing, you know, two roosters in the hen yard, newcomer on my patch and all that, but he's hardly a rooster. Everyone I know thinks he's gay. Not that it matters one way or another to me. It's a gut feeling, Olympia. Don't trust him, OK? Or at least be careful what you tell him."

Olympia held her coffee up to her nose and inhaled. The smell was heavenly. It was the first real coffee she'd had since she arrived on the island. While she swirled and sniffed the contents of her cup, she was asking herself how exactly she should respond to this. *Neutrally.*

"You're not out of line, Jack, you are expressing an opinion. I'm new here, and I didn't know a soul in the church or on the island, but I heard what you said, and I thank you for your concern. Of course, anything said here stays here."

Olympia leaned back in her chair and swiveled so they were facing each other. She didn't tell Jack he wasn't the only one who had reservations about William Bateson, but she prudently decided to change the subject.

"How is Janney feeling this morning?"

"Oh, fine," said Jack peeling the plastic cover away from the top of his own coffee cup. "She never has a hangover. I don't know how she does it with what she puts away, but she almost always wakes up ready to go on a moment's notice."

Olympia picked up her muffin and was methodically stripping the sticky paper away from the bottom. "A lot of alcoholics don't have hangovers. According to some experts it's one of the seven deadly signs. Maybe they just never sober up enough to have one."

Jack was dodging the real subject of the visit, and they both knew it.

Olympia put down her coffee. "So tell me, Jack, what about you? When and how are you going to tell Janney?"

The man across from her stared down into his lap.

"I haven't given myself much time. Today is Thursday, and I have to go into Boston on Monday—Sunday night really. They expect me to be in the hospital at six in the morning. I think that's cruel and abusive, but condemned men don't have much say in these matters."

"For heaven's sake, Jack, you are not condemned. You might be seriously ill, but you won't know the extent of anything until you have the procedure and they actually go in and look." Olympia spoke more sharply that she intended, and the anxious man looked up with a start and then nodded in resigned agreement.

"So until we know for sure, let's concentrate on two things. The first is keeping as positive an attitude as you possibly can, meaning whatever is going on, you are going to fight back like hell. And the second is telling your wife, who may or may not be able to help. So I guess we have a third issue, and that is, you may have to face this without her. She may totally freak out when she hears the news. Most alcoholics drink because life is just too painful to face without booze. Your situation is going to seriously rock an unstable boat, but you can't not tell her. How and when is the question before us."

Jack crossed his legs and leaned back in his chair. "Don't think I haven't thought of that. I guess that's probably one reason why I haven't told her. Here's what you don't know, Olympia. Our only son was killed in a skiing accident almost ten years ago. That's when the drinking got out of hand. I don't think she can take anything else."

"Oh, God, I am so sorry. That's awful." Olympia's thoughts flashed for an instant to her own two sons, *to all of her children* and how fiercely she loved them. His pain had to be unimaginable. "But Jack, what about you? Your loss is as great as hers. You are having to bear your grief alone."

"I learned to be tough," he said quietly. "I didn't have a choice, it was either that or lose my wife, too. The happy-flirty-Jack mask covers a lot, Olympia. You are one of the few I've ever let look behind it."

"Who else?"

"I have a little sister."

"I didn't know that either. Have you told her yet?"

"Yup. Called her the minute I got the diagnosis." Jack nodded and took a sip of his coffee. "She lives in L.A. She's a doctor. She's flying in tomorrow. She knows everything, Janney, the booze, our son, and now the cancer. She knows things even before I tell her. She's my twin—five minutes younger than me. That's what makes her the little sister. It's our twin-joke."

Olympia blew out a long sigh of relief.

"So you are not totally alone. Would it help to have her there when you tell Janney?"

Jack nodded. "That's the plan. Melody, that's her name, knows all the medical terms and what they mean, and she knows Janney. In spite of the booze, Melody and Janney really get along. Allan, that was our son, he really loved her, too. Called her his A.M., for Auntie Melody. It was their little joke. She was as devastated as we were when he was killed She doesn't have any kids. She never married."

Olympia looked at the man seated before her and wondered how much a single human being could take. She would do her best to help, but in less than eight weeks how much could she really do? Could she do anything at all? Olympia realized that despite the dramatic intensity of the last three days, she already cared about these people. She wanted to be there for them, for Jack and Janney right now and for Dory and Julia and Leigh—for all of them.

The telephone jangled its unpleasant way into the silence between, and Olympia let the machine answer it. It was a routine call about the time of the service on Sunday, and the recorded voice did everything that was necessary.

"When tomorrow is Melody arriving?"

"She flies into Logan Airport on the red eye at 7:00 a.m., and then she's going to take a Cape Air flight down here. Have you ever flown on one of those things? They've got a great safety record. Most of the ones that come here are nine-seaters, and one of those nine seats is beside the pilot. They are not for the faint hearted or the readily nauseous. I speak from experience."

Olympia vowed on the spot, safety record or not, never to include Cape Air on her list of island experiences. She had been known to throw up on a merry-go-round.

Jack had moved them deftly out of the seriousness of his situation and was making ready to go, gathering up his hardly touched coffee and the other muffin.

"Hey, you want this?" He held out the other muffin. Despite its lack of fat and calories and the politically correct raisins, he was right. They were delicious. She accepted and told him that she would enjoy it later, then stood and held out her hand.

"Thank you, Olympia. Talking about it doesn't really change anything. I still have cancer, and on Monday I'm going to find out how bad it is, but ... I guess I don't feel so alone with it any more. You're a good listener. So is my sister. I think you two are going to hit it off." Jack took her extended hand and held it in both of his. "Thank you for this, Reverend."

"I look forward to meeting your sister. If you feel you want to, let me know how the conversation with Janney goes."

"I'll call you after I talk to Janney, and I'll have Melody call you from Boston after the procedure and we know more about what's going on."

"I'll pray for you, Jack."

Olympia walked with Jack to the front door of the church and stood there until he drove away. As she turned to go back to the office, she heard the telephone ringing again and the answering machine coming on. This time the caller didn't hang up after the message.

"This is William Bateson speaking. I'm trying to reach Olympia Brown. It's urgent. I need ..."

Olympia reached down and picked up the receiver. "This is Olympia. Is something wrong? How can I help you?"

"Well, there's a bit of luck. Hello, Olympia. Let me get right to the point. I think I might have left a folder at Dory's house last night. I may have left it on the stairs or in the kitchen. It was dark when I left, so it's likely I didn't see where I left it. I really need it. You didn't find it, did you, maybe pick it up for safe keeping?"

"Actually, I picked up a whole bunch of folders including one I found on the stairs. After everybody left I went around the place and opened a few windows to let in fresh air. When I went into the guest room, I saw some file folders on a desk in there. They seemed to be Dory's household records, so I took them with me. I figured she might need them when the insurance people come today, and I didn't want them to get damp and maybe stick together. As I was leaving, I remembered the one on the stairs and went back for it. That must be the one you're talking about. I guess that's a long way of saying, yes, I've got it."

Olympia was fiddling nervously with the pencils in the jelly jar beside the phone.

"Did you happen to look inside?"

"I did, actually, just to see what it was. I didn't really read it. When I saw what was inside, I figured it was none of my business, so I closed it back up; but she really is thinking about selling."

"You didn't look through the whole thing then?" His voice sounded strained.

"No, like I said, I figured it was personal. Maybe you could come over this afternoon when the insurance adjusters are there, and I can give it back to you then. Come to think of it, with you being in real estate and all, we could probably use your help. Poor Dory. She's a strong lady, but this would knock anyone off their pins."

"She's less strong than you think, Reverend. Since I joined the church I've gotten to know her pretty well. She's definitely failing. The water is the most recent evidence of it. There have been any number of other little lapses I've covered up for her. Because you're her minister, I don't mind telling you that I'm worried about her. She really should sell that house of hers and get out before anything worse happens. But let's keep this between us for now. Later, if she does have to move, I think you would be the best person to be her advocate and help her make that decision."

"I appreciate your sharing this with me, William. I know Dory is very fond of you, and of course, I'll keep what you've said in confidence. I'm about to call her daughter. I think she needs to come and see to her mother."

"Do you really think that is necessary? I mean, couldn't we handle it through the church and all? What's to do? Clean up and settle the insurance and get her to a safe place. Between us we can do that. Why bother the daughter? She lives way out in Washington State. It's a long trip."

"It's very generous of you, William, but this really is a family matter. We have to call her. Whether she decides to come out here is up to her. I'm sure you're right. We probably could handle it ourselves, but the decision is for Dory and her daughter to make. I'll keep you posted."

"I'll come by your place this afternoon and pick up the folder. Goodbye, Reverend."

Fourteen

After the emotionally charged events of the morning, the rest of Olympia's time in the office was blessedly dull. She poked around the tiny office, locating some things, straightening others and answering routine phone calls, but she could not stop thinking about Jack Winters. By now she had completely revised her first impression of him. In the beginning she thought him to be a shallow, trust-funded idler with a roving eye and an alcoholic wife. Olympia had been right about the alcoholic wife part but realized she had been taken in by the façade that Jack chose to present to her and the rest of the world. The real Jack seemed to be a decent guy struggling in difficult circumstances without much support. That he was financially well off played no part in his present distress. She was comforted knowing his twin sister Melody would be there to help and looked forward to meeting her.

Leaning forward in the creaky chair and rearranging pencils for the third time, Olympia realized she was struggling with something else as well—and that was William Bateson. Something slipped through a crack in his polished veneer when he asked her about the missing papers, something dark, maybe even threatening, in the tone of his voice. She heard it again when she told him she was going to call Dory's daughter. What did it mean? Maybe Julia Scott-Norton was right, maybe he did bear watching. On the other hand, he seemed to be genuinely concerned for Dory, and she certainly appeared to trust him.

Olympia decided she needed to have a look through the folder in question. In fact, since she had told William when she would be home, maybe she should go home early so she could read through it without interruption. If the man had not been so emphatic about its whereabouts and return, she would never have given it a second thought. Now she was giving everything a second thought. *There is one hell of a lot more to this island than meets the eye. And pursuant to that, what will be the consequences of my trying to learn what it is?*

When she had accepted the offer of eight paid weeks as a summer minister on the Island of Martha's Vineyard, it had sounded like a gift from heaven. Now she wasn't so sure. It was only Thursday, four days after her Monday arrival, and she had yet to experience a peaceful and idyllic moment unless you counted sleeping. Even then she couldn't tell if it was idyllic or not. She was certainly going to learn a whole lot more about parish ministry than she had anticipated, and that would be a bonus. But this so-called time-out-of-time was beginning to look like a mixed blessing that only more time-out-of-time would define.

Life happens when you are making other plans.

She looked around the office and was getting ready to leave when the phone rang one more time. She waited until she heard the brisk, no nonsense voice of Julia Scott-Norton on the answering machine before lifting the receiver and identifying herself.

"Good morning, Julia, it's Olympia. I'm here looking through old Sunday bulletins and Parish Committee minutes. How's Dory?"

"She's fine. You know, sitting up and taking nourishment. But she's insisting that she didn't leave the water running." Julia dropped her voice and spoke the next few words quietly. "And you know what, Olympia? I'm inclined to believe her. She's never been one to make things up. In fact, just the opposite. She's a stickler for details."

"Well, then, how could it have happened?" asked Olympia, doodling red intersecting circles around the edges of an old pew card. "It's not like a pipe burst or anything, but then I came in after the fact, so I guess I don't really know. We can talk more about it this afternoon. What time are the insurance adjusters coming?"

"About two," said Julia. "Will you be able to be there? I've called her daughter Jessica. She's got a few things she has to finish up, but she's going to try and get here before Sunday."

"I'll be there at two," said Olympia, wistfully watching another un-idyllic day glide away from her like the outgoing tide, "and I'm glad you called her daughter. What does she do that she has to finish up?"

"Jessica West is an internationally recognized cellist; I'm surprised you haven't heard of her."

"Now that you say her name, of course I've heard of her." Olympia unconsciously pulled herself up to a more attentive position. "I paid a small fortune to hear her in person playing the Elgar cello concerto with the Boston Symphony. She's fantastic, but I would never have connected her with Dory."

"Jessica is just another islander as far as they both are concerned," said Julia comfortably. "She has played any number of benefit concerts here, and she's as modest as they come. I'll see you at two."

Julia rang off before Olympia could say any more. She knew that the island was home to any number of celebrities, and she secretly hoped she would meet one or two, but Jessica West? Wow! She might be an internationally recognized cellist, but she was also the concerned daughter of an aging woman who needed help. So much for the celebrated lives of the rich and famous. They put their socks on one at a time just like the rest of us. Olympia grinned as she replaced the church bulletins in the drawer and looked up at the clock. She had better get going if she was going to take a look at those papers. It was already after eleven.

She stood up, picked up the paper sack containing the muffin Jack Winters had left for her, walked into the bathroom and poured the remains of her coffee into the sink.

Six minutes after leaving the church, Olympia unlocked the door to her cottage. Although it was closed up and therefore uncomfortably warm, she inhaled a deep homecoming breath and went around opening windows and greeting the cats. After that she sat down at the drop leaf table that was both dining table and writing desk. The folders were lying exactly where she had left them.

The top folder, labeled Household Expenses, contained a detailed record of just that, Dory's daily and monthly expenses. Each was neatly listed with the dates of bills received and paid carefully written in a clear, steady hand. There were no surprises here.

The next one was labeled Tradesmen and held a list of plumbers, electricians and heating people with telephone numbers and annotated with comments like, "does not return calls," or "is always late," or "good when you can get him." Olympia smiled and picked up the third folder of the five she had in her lap. In it was a handwritten obituary and plans for her memorial service along with her Life Crisis File and a signed and notarized durable power of attorney naming her daughter Jessica. Slipped in with this was a signed advanced medical directive. This folder she'd labeled Afterthoughts.

Olympia's eyes filled with tears despite the humor. Dory was so practical, and Olympia knew she would do anything for her. She just hoped it would not be her funeral, at least not now and preferably not ever. Olympia shook off the wave of sadness and picked up another folder.

This one was labeled Christmas Past and Presents, and in it were the names of people to whom she evidently gave gifts. After each name was a description of the gift and year it was given—presumably, thought Olympia, so she wouldn't repeat herself.

There was nothing wrong with this lady.

Olympia looked at her watch; it was almost noon. If she was going to look at everything in that folder of Bateson's, she needed to do it before he got there.

From the outside it looked like the others, a plain beige manila file folder, but inside, to her dismay, Olympia found an approved plot plan of Dory's property, a photograph of the front of her house, clear pictures of all the rooms and a detailed drawing of each level of the house, including the basement. On a separate sheet was a penciled draft of an advertisement written on Gingerbread Homes Realty stationery which read: "Priced for quick sale, lovely historic Island property, owner needs to downsize, this is a must see …"

Olympia was prevented from any further reading by an impatient knock at the door and the sound of William Bateson calling her name.

"Be right there." She was careful to straighten the papers before opening the door.

For reasons she couldn't name, she didn't want the man in her house. She stood in the doorway with one hand on the doorknob and the other holding the folder against her chest.

"As I said on the phone, I thought it was another one of hers. Once I opened it and looked inside I knew it had to be the one you were looking for. So is she really going to sell?"

William Bateson never missed a beat. "Nothing is signed yet, Olympia. I would never rush anyone into selling their home. You'll just have to trust me on that, but we have talked about it, and I did start a file for her if or when she does make the decision. When these old ones make up their minds to do something, they want it all done yesterday. Better a person she knows and trusts than some stranger intent on scoring a sleeper on the housing market."

Olympia wasn't so sure about that but said nothing other than, "So has she seen all of this? What does she think?"

He hesitated. "Well, not exactly all of it. The old ones get confused when you give them too much paperwork up front. I took the liberty of getting it together for when, or if, she's ready. We have talked about it. I believe in being prepared, don't you, Reverend Brown?" *There's that tone of voice again.*

"Whenever and however I can, Mr. Bateson. I'm sure her daughter Jessica will want to have some say in all of this, especially if it concerns the house she grew up in."

"You can be sure I'll make a point of sitting down with her myself and getting her thoughts on the matter."

Olympia held out the papers. "That's probably a good idea. Meanwhile, I need a few minutes to grab some lunch and freshen up before the insurance people arrive. Are you planning to be there this afternoon?"

"I'm not sure. I have a meeting at the office. I can always check with her later."

"Might help if you were."

"Well, if you put it that way, I'll make a point of it."

Olympia nodded and then shut and locked the door.

A little later, as she was putting away her lunch dishes, she heard the voice of Julia Scott-Norton through the open window. "The insurance adjusters are here, Olympia."

The gentle command was implicit, but right now, Olympia was more than grateful for Julia's inborn authority. She followed Julia across the grass and up the steps to Dory's bright purple front door.

Inside, Dory was sitting on the sofa looking anxious but in control. Next to her sat William Bateson, and across from her was a man who, upon her entrance, stood and held out a card. "I'm Mike Barnes, Insurance Adjuster, Cape and Islands Finance Collaborative, and you are?"

Olympia took the card and looked at it before answering. "I'm Olympia Brown, the summer minister at the church around the corner, Dory's church. I'm staying in her rental cottage next door."

"Pleasedt'meetcha," said Barnes in a single run-on word. "Call me Mike."

Olympia stepped over a pile of wet things on the floor and took a seat. "Let me know how I can help."

"There won't be much any of us can do right now," said Julia, taking over the conversation. "These two need to look around and make a list of loss and damage, and then when Dory's daughter Jessica arrives we can go over it again and come to some kind of an agreement. When we do, then we can settle on a final amount."

"We all?" asked Mike Barnes, looking at the woman in front of him.

"We all," repeated Julia for emphasis. We are a church family here, and we do everything together, don't we Dory?"

Dory leaned back against the cushions of the sofa, breathed out a gentle sigh and smiled her agreement. William Bateson, who had been mostly silent, turned to Dory and said, "You can count me in on that, too. You know how I feel about Mrs. West, don't you, Julia?"

Fifteen

Later that day, after the insurance adjuster was finished with the house inspection, and he and Bateson had left, Julia and Olympia set about gathering some more of Dory's clothing and personal things. On the pretext of needing help, Olympia called Julia upstairs where Dory couldn't hear them, saying she needed an extra hand carrying some things. When they were alone in Dory's bedroom, Olympia made a lot of noise opening and shutting doors and dresser drawers while beckoning with a wave of her hand for Julia to come closer.

Olympia spoke in an urgent whisper to the one woman she dared tell about what she had discovered. "You may be right about William Bateson."

Julia turned her head sharply toward Olympia, giving her full attention.

"What do you mean?"

"Last night after everyone left, I went around opening windows and checking things. I found a folder on the stairs. I figured it was Dory's, so I picked it up and took it along with the others I took from her desk upstairs. I wanted to keep them from getting damp. I planned to give them to her today in case she needed the information for the insurance people."

"And?" said Julia.

"There were a total of five folders. Four of them were Dory's household records and personal information, all very clear and meticulous but ..." Olympia paused

"And the fifth one, what was in the fifth one?" said Julia.

Olympia took a deep breath. "The fifth one was a folder containing pictures, photographs and drawings. There was even a draft copy of a newspaper advertisement announcing the sale of Dory's house, printed on Gingerbread Realty Stationery."

"Julia's eyes went wide. "Where is it now? I want to have a look at it."

"William Bateson has it. He called me at the church and asked if I'd found it. What else could I do? Until I looked, I had no idea what was in it. He said that Dory was only thinking about selling, and of course he was going to talk to the daughter. On one hand he sounds sincere and business-like, and on the other ... well, there's just something about him. Maybe it's nothing, but ever since you told me to keep an eye on him I don't feel I can trust him."

They both heard Dory call up from the living room. "Are you two OK up there I don't need that much, you know."

"We're on our way down," said Julia. "Do you want your perfume?"

"Just the Yardley's."

Olympia smiled and went over to the dresser and picked up the bottle of English Lavender. It had been a favorite of her grandmother. She remembered picking up a small round crystal bottle with a rubber squeeze bulb atomizer in Grandmother's bedroom. Now, smelling the lavender, she was inhaling the smell of her grandmother, the one who smoked Camels in a pearl and ebony cigarette holder, drank coffee by the quart, and made special M&M cookies just for her.

"Here, you carry these, and I'll carry the rest." Julia's efficiency brought Olympia instantly back to the present. "Look, why don't you get in your car and follow me home. We'll get Dory settled, then go someplace where we can talk."

"I think that's a very good idea," said Olympia.

~

Less than three miles away from where Julia and Olympia were gathering up Dory's things in preparation for settling her into Julia's place, William Bateson and two other men were seated around a table in the back room of an intentionally charming, pink and white Victorian cottage. It was conveniently near, but not actually in, the fabled Methodist campground in Oak Bluffs. The West file lay open in front of them on a shabby-chic, painted wooden table that underscored the Carpenter Gothic ambiance of Gingerbread Realty Associates.

Hunched forward, leaning on his elbows, William Bateson, with his sleeves rolled up and his tie over the back of the chair he was seated on, took a long, noisy swallow of a Diet Coke before speaking to the other two men in the room.

"I think that minister woman's going to be trouble. How the hell could I have been so stupid as to leave that folder where she could find it?"

Al Francis tapped the end of his pencil on the open file. "Maybe we should just cut bait and get out of here. You know I'm a little leery about this one. On the other hand, if you are really as far along as you say you are, Billy-boy, then maybe we just hang tight and lay low until the preacher-lady is out of here. What did you say, eight weeks? We could hit and run right after that. It would be inconvenient, to say the least, if she started asking questions and poking around. We wouldn't want her to turn up anything that could, uh, shall I say, reflect badly on us."

"Look, Al, I'm going to stick with the church-going, slightly swishy real estate agent helping the old lady act. It works every time. Just because I happen to be a realtor, and the old lady said she wanted to sell her house doesn't make me a person of interest. I'm just doing my job. But I'm going to sort of step back and not do it for a while, OK? I'll wait until the daughter gets here. Then if I have to shift gears, I will. I've done this before, remember?"

William Bateson and Al Francis turned to the third man in the room, Mike Barnes, Insurance Adjuster. These three plus Mary Beth Lessing, who had called in to say she'd been delayed, were the Gingerbread Men Associates.

Barnes got up and went over to the mini-fridge in the corner of the room. He was so tall he had to bend almost double to see inside. "Anyone want a beer? The way I see it, we just have to be careful for a little while. We know how to do this. After I lowball the insurance estimate and make it all sound really complicated, I tell her it's going to be really drawn out, and she can't possibly move back there until it's fixed. The old ones just can't handle the disruption and the confusion of all that legal stuff. That's when you come back on the scene, Sir William Bateson to the rescue, and help her sort it all out. "

"Grab me some ice, will you?" said Bateson, swirling the remains of his drink in a warm glass. "All this heat makes Willie B. a thirsty boy."

Mike Barnes handed several dripping ice cubes to Bateson, who dropped them into his glass, wiped his dripping hand on his pants leg and nodded his thanks.

"The revised plan is for you to continue being useful around the church, lay off the old lady, make friends with the daughter, and wait until the Reverend Ms. Trouble gets her butt off the island. Then we're home free."

"And if we're not home free, as you so coyly put it?" said William, draining the last of his Coke and making a great show of examining the bottom of the glass.

"Accidents happen," said Barnes, picking up the folder and putting it into the file drawer marked Pending and slamming it shut. "Just make sure the poor old dear signs on the dotted line first."

Sixteen

Julia parked her van as close to the house as she could, and Olympia pulled the vintage Volvo in right behind her. The day was warm, but a big tree that had been growing outside the kitchen door for over a hundred years would shade their comings and goings as they unloaded Dory and her boxes and bags into the comfortable old house. She was showing the strain, and both women knew she didn't need to add heat stroke to her list of woes. Within a half hour she was settled in, and the three of them were seated in rocking chairs on the porch, sipping glasses of iced tea.

"What do you think will happen next?" Dory was chewing on the sprig of fresh mint that Julia had tucked into each of their dripping glasses.

"Well," said Julia, "I never had a flood, but we did have some storm damage a few years ago. Part of that big old tree by the back door came down in Hurricane Bob and smashed up a good part of the corner of the house. What a mess that was. After it fell it kept on raining and blowing, so I guess there was water damage, too, now that I think of it … but listen to me, I'm meandering all over the place." Julia laughed comfortably at herself and addressed Dory's question.

"Usually, it doesn't take all that long. Depends on the company, really. This Barnes person is not an islander, so I don't know. But back to the point again. The insurance people will send you an estimate of what they think repair and replacement costs will be, and if you agree, you sign it and they get started."

"Actually," said Olympia, leaning forward and putting her glass on the railing, then wiping the back of her neck with a paper napkin. "I believe I heard Mike Barnes say that you could begin necessary repairs any time. Just keep the receipts. He said something about doing what any responsible home owner would do to protect the property from further damage. So I guess you could get started calling people tomorrow."

"Oh, dear," said Dory, "I wouldn't know where to begin, who to call or what to ..." She stopped in mid-sentence, and in that moment she looked all of her frail eighty-four years.

Olympia looked up at Julia and moved her head from side to side in an almost imperceptible gesture of concern and sympathy, then reached over and took Dory's hand in hers.

"Don't even think about it, Dory. Julia and I can go back and see if anything needs immediate attention, and if it does, we'll take care of it. If not, we can wait until your daughter gets here. We'll call the carpet people to come get the rugs and keep the windows open to dry out the house as much as possible. I don't think there was any structural damage. What else is there to think about?"

"Right now, I don't think I could tell you. Do you mind if I go lie down? I think I need to." Dory set down her glass and pushed herself up on the broad arms of the rocking chair.

"Are you OK?" asked Julia, reaching out a reassuring hand to the weary old woman.

"Not really." Dory was twisting her worn wedding band on her knobby finger. "My house got flooded, and I don't think I did it even though it looks like I did. And much as I appreciate this, Julia, I would rather be in my own bed than yours, and I have no idea when that is going to be. So to answer your question, no, I'm not all right, but I'm as good as I can be, considering everything."

She reached out to steady herself on the railing of the porch. "I need to get my sea legs under me before I take the first step. At my age I can't risk a fall. That's all I'd need."

Julia and Olympia waited until they heard the door to her room click shut before resuming their conversation.

Olympia retrieved her glass from the railing and turned to Julia. "So what do you think?"

"I think the poor thing has had enough for ten people to deal with, and if she seems a little overwhelmed, she has every reason to be. I think we just take care of her, give her lots of TLC until Jessica gets here, and then we make some decisions. We can arrange for cleaning out the worst of it. Dory is not without money, you know, she's just quiet about it. If she wanted to, she could bulldoze the house and build a new one three times bigger, just like that." Julia snapped her fingers.

Olympia shook her head in surprise. "I wouldn't have thought she was wealthy. Just the opposite. She lives so simply. Things are patched and worn. Clean as a whistle, but everything I saw was well used."

Julia chuckled. It was a pleasant, rich sound. "Islanders do not make an ostentatious display of their financial standing. It's just not done. In fact, it's quite the opposite. Some people positively work at looking downright ratty when in fact they could buy and sell any dozen of us put together."

"I guess I have a lot to learn," said Olympia.

"For less than a week here, I'd say you are doing just fine. But before you go, I need to talk to you about the funeral for Mary Parker. Her son called me last night. They plan to have her cremated as soon as her body is released and then have a simple graveside ceremony followed by a huge lunch at the P.A. Club. That's what she wanted. Mary Parker absolutely loved going out to lunch."

"P.A. Club?"

"The Portuguese American Club, it's near the cemetery in Oak Bluffs."

"Parker isn't a Portuguese name is it?"

"Not at all," said Julia, "but it's a great place for a party. Dan Parker, that's her son, is planning to call you over the weekend. I gave him your cell phone number. I hope you don't mind."

The truth was, Olympia did mind. It was a private thing, and she preferred to make that decision herself, but she said, "Perhaps you should give me his number, as well. I left my cell phone at home in Brookfield. My friend Frederick will be bringing it down with him this weekend."

"You have a friend named Frederick?"

"He's English," said Olympia.

Later that evening, alone in her cottage, Olympia did manage to make serious headway on her sermon for the coming Sunday and still have enough time left over to call Frederick, using Dory's extension phone, and catch up on the news from Brookfield. Their conversation moved from the logistics of his getting there that Saturday, to her concerns about Dory, to what in the world she might say and do when she met with her daughter. With that out of the way, they spent the rest of the time describing how delicious it was going to be when the two of them had a nice soft horizontal surface on which to reacquaint themselves. While it wasn't exactly telephone sex, it definitely bordered on long-distance foreplay.

On Saturday morning Olympia collected Frederick from the ferry in Vineyard Haven at eight in the morning and went straight back home. A little after midday, the two of them set off, pink cheeked and ravenous, in search of some lunch. With their energy restored, they meandered up and down Main Street, investigating the colorful shops, slurping gigantic ice cream cones, and acting like any other tourists who were totally enchanted with the charm and ambience of the island.

Frederick offered to come to church with her on Sunday, but Olympia declined, saying that since she hadn't been in a pulpit in a long time she might be too distracted if the object of her affection was sitting in the congregation, grinning at her. So Frederick, kind heart that he was, agreed to stay home, talk to the cats, and have lunch ready for her when she returned.

On Sunday afternoon Frederick and Olympia were seated knee to knee on her postage stamp deck, enjoying the lunch Frederick had concocted in her absence. While they were eating their egg salad sandwiches, he asked her about the church and the congregation and how she liked parish ministry so far. He then moved on to the more tender subject of how she was feeling about going into Boston the next day to meet her daughter, and finally, what was happening with the house and the lady next door. Taking the items in reverse order, Olympia began with the flood.

"Everything to do with repairing or selling the house is on hold, as far as I know. The insurance adjuster was here the day after it happened, and he hasn't gotten back to anyone yet. Dory's daughter Jessica will be coming out from Seattle next week, and then I suspect things will start moving forward. All the poor thing wants is to get back to her own place, but she can't until we get it cleaned up a little more. Right now, it's not safe. Who knows what structural damage the water did? It is an old house, and we both know what old houses are like."

Frederick nodded and held out the plate of sandwich halves. Olympia picked up the nearest one. "Nice touch, my dear, the sprinkling of parsley on top. I like parsley. Anyway, Mrs. West was in church this morning. Everybody wanted to help her, but there's nothing to be done until we get the figures from the adjuster. Nobody is supposed to go in there until the town building inspector gives the OK."

"Well, then, that's odd."

"What do you mean?"

"While I was puttering around this morning, making lunch and hosing down the bedroom in case of fire …" Olympia blushed and giggled. "I saw a man go into the house. He looked over in this direction, but your car wasn't here, and I was behind the curtain, so I'm sure he thought no one was home, not that it mattered, but he did look and …"

"Frederick, get to the point. What did he do? What did he look like?"

"Well, it was obvious he had his own key, and after he went inside I don't know what he did, because I couldn't see him. But I do remember what he looked like. He was medium height, light complexion, dark hair, clean shaven and wearing a suit and tie. I only noticed because his tie matched his pocket handkerchief. I didn't think people did that any more. Kind of old fashioned, isn't it?"

"Damn! It had to be William Bateson."

"I love it when you talk dirty. Who's William Bateson?"

Olympia chuckled despite the sudden gravity of the situation. "William Bateson is a member of the congregation, and he was late for church this morning. He's a realtor, and he's been very attentive to Mrs. West, my landlady. Julia Scott-Norton, she's the board president, has her doubts about him, and I'm kind of on the fence. I can't say I like him, but on the other hand, I don't dislike him. Let's just say that he's not given me any real reason not to trust him—so far, anyway."

Frederick picked up another sandwich half and raised a quizzical eyebrow as Olympia continued.

"I mean, if he is a real estate agent by profession, then he's a perfect person to help Mrs. West if she wants to sell. But I think there's some confusion as to whether or not she really wants to sell. The board president thinks she just likes to talk about selling. She also thinks that Mr. Bateson might be pressuring her. Then the flood happened, and now everything is in limbo until we hear from the insurance adjusters and her daughter gets here."

"Well, then, to go back to my original question, what would he be doing in Mrs. West's house if everything is on hold?"

"That, my gallant Englishman, is precisely what I want to find out right now. Maybe nothing, maybe getting information for the insurance adjuster, maybe reassessing how much she can get if she sells. But there's only one way to find out."

Olympia collected the remains of their lunch, stashed it all on the doll-sized countertop beside the equally miniscule sink and marched out the door with a sputtering Frederick following close behind.

"Do you have a key?"

"No, but I know where she keeps it. Everybody here keeps an extra key under a rock or a flowerpot beside one or both of the doors. That way we all know how to get in if we need to."

"Do you keep a key outside your door like that?" asked Frederick.

"No!"

Olympia lifted said flowerpot, removed the key and opened the front door to Dory's house. Despite the open windows, it was beginning to smell moldy. She wrinkled her nose and started looking around.

"I don't see anything different since the last time I was here."

"What about upstairs?" Frederick walked to the foot of the sharply angled staircase. The wet boards squeaked under his feet.

"I'll run upstairs and check," said Olympia. "You stay here; no reason for both of us to go."

Olympia gave Frederick a friendly pat on the behind as she passed by him and started up the stairs. As she ascended she remembered slipping on the pencil the other night and was now taking great care as to where she put her feet. She was almost to the top when, without warning, the entire stair tread came loose and went out from under her. Olympia twisted crazily and grabbed for the hand rail. Miraculously, she caught herself two steps down.

"Jesus Christ!"

"Crikey, Olympia, are you all right?' Frederick was up the stairs and kneeling beside her in the time it took for Olympia to gasp a second time.

"I think I'm all right. The stair tread came loose. I could have broken my leg."

Olympia was feeling her various movable body parts and came to the decision that she would be sore as hell tomorrow, and she would probably have some spectacular bruises on her leg and hip where she hit, but other than that, thanks to her quick reaction in grabbing the rail, she was basically unharmed. She was, however, badly shaken and remained seated on the stairs.

"Frederick, that could have been Dory. If this happened to her, she might have killed herself. Old people die in falls. These are really steep stairs."

"Do you suppose the tread came loose because of the water?"

"The water didn't get up this high, Frederick. It was all on the ground floor. Maybe the extreme dampness loosened something."

"Can you get up by yourself? I want to have a look at that tread. I think you're sitting on it."

Olympia pulled herself up and crept down the stairs. Already, she was beginning to hurt. "I think I'd better get a couple of band aids. I've got a pretty good scrape on my shin. All in all, I'd say I'm a bit of a mess, my dear."

"Olympia? Come here and look at this." Frederick was holding out the stair tread for her inspection. "I know this is an old house, but it's clearly a well-built house. I don't think this stair tread came loose by itself. Look here, I think somebody may have pried it loose."

"Let's take it back to my place where we can examine it. But before we do, maybe you can put some sort of a barrier at the bottom of the stairs so no one else gets hurt."

Seventeen

Later that day Olympia considered calling Julia and telling her about the stair tread, but upon reflection she decided that this might be something she would rather show her in person. This left her with patching up her cuts and bruises and thinking about the following day, when she would see her daughter for the second time in her life. *Oh, God, what am I going to wear?*

Wonderful as he was, Frederick was a man, and by the casual, bordering-on-eccentric way he turned himself out, she knew he would be useless in terms of helping her choose an outfit. She stood in front of the shoebox-sized clothes closet and pulled out a pair of white slacks and some comfortable, light-toned walking shoes. To this she added an oversized, pale turquoise blouse that would keep her cool if the day turned out hot and would gracefully camouflage the womanly breadth of her hips and tummy. To anyone but Frederick, she had the appearance of a woman methodically preparing for a trip into the big city. In truth, she was a wreck, and they both knew it. But having something to do and having Frederick there with her, providing tea and wine at appropriate intervals, was helping to pass the time until they could go to bed. Not surprisingly, Olympia had neither the mood nor the energy for any bedroom gymnastics, and to her amazement she fell asleep almost instantly.

The next morning she was far too anxious to eat, but Frederick managed to persuade her to nibble a banana while they were pacing around the ferry and later brought her a cup of peppermint tea to calm her stomach. It took some convincing, but he finally persuaded her to let him accompany her and then to stand at a respectful distance when she met with her daughter. At first Olympia had refused the offer, but then she realized she might need someone with her when it was over. In so doing she realized that she was beginning to trust this man, or perhaps she was beginning to trust herself. Either or both would remain to be seen, but at this juncture she was deeply grateful.

Before they left the house that morning, Olympia called Julia to try and find a time when they might meet, but she was already out. She left a message on Julia's machine, saying only that she would be away for the day and would return that evening, and could they find a time to talk about the Parker funeral and a few other things that had come up since last they'd last met.

The ferry ride was uneventful, and the bus to Boston was waiting for them as scheduled. Once on board and seated, the teddy bear she had picked for her expected grandchild proved to be as much of a comfort to herself as she hoped it would be in the future to a child she could only hope she would know. She sat, staring out the window, rubbing a fuzzy ear and counting the mile markers into Boston.

When they arrived at South Station, a grand old Victorian landmark in the center of the city, Olympia was moving like a mechanical doll. In one way she was so full of emotions that she felt she might shatter if someone so much as nudged her. At the same time she felt like an automaton, putting one foot ahead of the other, looking neither left nor right, mindlessly moving forward toward her destination, clutching her teddy. The last part of the journey took them on a red train to Park Street Station, then up what seemed like a million steps to the Boston Common.

Having grown up in the Boston area, the Common, as most people called it, was familiar territory. But today she remembered little. She walked along the curving paths, praying she would say the right things. Frederick walked several feet behind her and planned to sit somewhere nearby on a bench. He had brought along a book and a crossword and a recent edition of *The Guardian*. He assured her he was well supplied with things to do and not to give him a second thought.

Olympia stationed herself on a wooden bench beside the lagoon in the shade of a large oak and waited, looking at the people walking by for what might be a familiar face.

"Olympia Brown?"

"Laura?"

Oh, my God, here she is. This grown woman is my daughter.

Olympia nodded and crushed the teddy to her chest as she held out her free hand to the woman standing in front of her. She was lovely, slightly shorter than Olympia with straight, shoulder-length, light brown hair. She was wearing oversized sun glasses, so Olympia couldn't see her eyes. She remembered they were blue when Laura was born, but then all newborn's eyes are sort of bluish.

"Um, you want to walk a little bit, or would you like to sit on one of the benches?" Laura looked briefly at her mother and then glanced off to the side, not quite making eye contact.

"Uh, sure, I mean, if you want to, or we could go for a coffee or … Oh, God, Laura, I've dreamed about this moment for thirty-five years, and I'm totally tongue tied — and I talk for a living. Go figure."

Laura smiled and reached for her mother's arm. "Let's go for a ride on the swan boats. Can you believe I've lived here all my life, and I've never actually done it? When I was little, my mother read me the book *Make Way for Ducklings* a thousand times. I even had a little ducky-toy, but I never actually got onto one of the boats."

Olympia winced at Laura's use of the word "mother." She blinked her eyes several times and allowed herself to be led onto the deck of one of Boston's most beloved and historic tourist attractions. Because it was a Monday morning, there were not many people waiting in the ticket line, and she and her daughter had the front row bench all to themselves. When they pushed off, Olympia turned to Laura and handed her the bear.

"I told you I'd be carrying it, it's for the baby. You're not showing at all. When is it due? Do you know yet what it is?"

"The baby is due in late October or early November. I've decided not to ask what the sex is, although I could change my mind. It would be easier to know what color to paint the room."

They both laughed at that.

"There is so much I want to ask you, Laura, and you probably feel the same way. I may be a minister, but that doesn't carry much water when you are the one in the middle of a crisis."

"Since when is this a crisis?"

"Laura, this is an earthquake and a tornado and a blizzard all rolled into one. It is something I have prayed for from the moment they took you away from me, but now that you are actually here in front of me, I haven't a clue as to where to begin."

The sway of the boat and the friendly chatter of the ducks paddling alongside, begging for food, began to ease the tension between the two women.

"So let's begin at the beginning, you first. Please tell me about the day of my birth, and if you don't mind, I want to know who my father was — or is. For a long time I didn't think I ever wanted to know either of you. I've been curious about him, but I was furious with you. But now, seeing you here, actually sitting beside you, pregnant with your grandchild … I want to know my birth mother."

When Olympia finished wiping her eyes and blowing her nose, and nodding a silent affirmative to Frederick, who was now standing on the bridge as they passed under it, she did just that. The story was not an unfamiliar one. Nice girl, middle class background, everything going for her, met up with an equally nice boy at an interfaith youth conference. He was from Oregon, attending Northeastern University on the co-op plan, and she fell hopelessly and incautiously in love with him.

"His name was David Pearlstein, and would you believe I never even actually had sex with him? But I learned the hard way that in rare instances, close enough is all it takes, and in my case, unfortunately — or maybe very fortunately — it was. Of course, no one believed me, least of all David. He accused me of being with someone else and literally left me crying my eyes out on Huntington Avenue in front of Symphony Hall. My mother, who, by the way, is still alive, doesn't know that I've reconnected with you, and quite frankly, I'm not sure when, or even if, I'm going to tell her.

"She didn't believe me either. She was furious. David took off for parts unknown, never to be seen again, and my mother sent me away to give birth and give you up with the dire warning that I could only come back home providing I never spoke of it again."

Now it was Laura's turn to wipe her eyes. She turned on the hard wooden bench and looked into her mother's eyes. "That's awful. What happened then?"

Olympia took a deep breath and continued. "I had no choice. I did what I was told and never heard from him again. Not once. I was heartbroken, disillusioned, humiliated and completely alone. Even though I wasn't Catholic, I was shipped off to a convent home for disgraced girls. I got good prenatal care, a lot of pitying looks, and delivered you without so much as an aspirin for the pain. They said that by feeling the pain we could partially atone for our sins. They let me hold you just one time, and when no one was looking, I christened you and named you Faith, using water from a plastic cup on the night table. Then I kissed your little red face, and they took you away. That's the quick version. There's more, but that's all I can manage for now. Even with you sitting here, I don't know if I'll ever get over seeing you being carried off in the arms of a stranger."

As the paddleboat passed under the stone bridge for a second time, Frederick looked down upon the two women sitting with their arms around each other and slowly swaying back and forth with the motion of the boat.

Later, on the bus ride back to the ferry, Olympia alternated between repeating word for word all that she and her daughter had said to one another and staring out of the window, watching the reflection of her own tears in the glass. Frederick offered his handkerchief and listened when she wanted to talk and simply held on to her hand when she didn't. Over the course of the trip he learned that Laura had been raised in the city of Winchester, just north of Boston. *So near and yet so far, just a bus ride from where I'd been teaching for almost thirty years.*

Laura was one of three children in a family of adopted siblings, two boys and herself. The couple that raised her were both professionals. Her father was a high school English teacher who played violin whenever he got the chance, and her mother was a pediatrician who, ironically, couldn't have children of her own. When, after all these years Laura decided to find her birth mother, it was her adoptive mother who helped her contact the department of records in Boston and went with her when she finally decided to go.

In the end both women agreed that it had been a hugely successful day and first meeting, so much so that Olympia decided that she could introduce Laura to Frederick, who just happened to have a camera stashed in his pocket and took their first-ever picture together. Before they parted Olympia and her daughter promised to keep in touch, and Laura asked Olympia if she would like to meet her parents. They both knew there was so much more to say and learn, but they agreed it would be best to save it for another day.

Late that afternoon, when Frederick and Olympia clomped their way up the metal gangway and onto the ferry, Olympia was two synapses short of being totally brain-dead. Frederick poured her into a seat and galloped off in search of a glass of wine. Anything that needed to be done could be taken care of the next day. When he returned holding the brimming plastic glass aloft, not spilling one precious pale drop, the words *life is what happens while you are making other plans* once again flashed through her mental mist. Olympia smiled as she held out her hand and gratefully accepted the wine.

February 27, 1861
On the twelfth of February, in the year eighteen sixty-one, in a prodigious snowstorm that brought everything in the city of Cambridge to a halt, my son was born. I confess before his birth to wishing that I might have a daughter in the belief that a daughter would be easier to raise on one's own. But when Jonathan Otis Winslow, howling louder than the wind outside the house, was placed in my weary arms, I was forever changed, and my new life began. To say that I am unprepared for this is an understatement, but his name means "God has given." I am in no doubt that if Jonathan has been given to me, then the selfsame God who blessed me with his healthy birth will surely give me strength to see this through.
More anon, LFW

Eighteen

On Tuesday morning, Olympia took Frederick to the ferry, bade him a fond farewell until the next time, and then began to walk up the main road toward the church. She needed to check her phone messages and see if she could come up with a sermon subject for that coming Sunday. Knowing that this would require coffee, she stopped at the Mug and Bagel and ordered a cappuccino and a cinnamon-raisin bagel with cream cheese.

Once in the office with her food and drink within reach on the desk in front of her, she listened to the messages. One wrong number, two calls about the time of the Sunday service, and a gentleman with a rather hoarse voice asking the minister to call Mr. Daniel Parker about a graveside service for his mother, Mrs. Mary Elgin Parker. Olympia remembered with an uncomfortable jolt that she was supposed to contact him over the weekend, but her daughter and all matters pertaining thereto had taken precedence.

She also wanted to call Jack Winters and see how he was doing but wondered if that might be too pushy. Perhaps it would be best for him to call her. She had told him he could when they'd talked last week. Then there was Dory and the matter of getting her back into her house and whether she would be selling it. *Better hold off until the daughter gets here for that.*

Olympia knew there was a clear line between pastoral interest and over-involvement, and she also knew that she was not always very good at drawing that line. This was so different from college chaplaincy — but that's what she was here for, to see if this was going to be the next phase of her professional life or not. She sipped her coffee and wiped the foam from the steamed milk off her upper lip. There had to be a way to drink cappuccino without wearing it, but she never seemed to know how to do that either.

She reached for the phone to call Julia Scott-Norton and tell her about the stair tread, then changed her mind. *I can't appear to be a busybody,* she thought. *This is their world not mine, and appearances to the contrary, Frederick might have been wrong. Maybe that stair tread just worked itself loose on its own.* Olympia lived in an old house, older than that one, and things were always coming to bits when she least expected it. She eyed the phone. Much as she wanted to, it was too soon to call her daughter. She knew they both needed to digest all that had happened.

That left Daniel Parker and his mother's funeral. She picked up the phone and dialed the number she'd written on the note pad beside the phone. The man who had left the message picked up and said, "Dan Parker."

"Oh, hello, this is Reverend Olympia Brown calling. I'm the summer minister at the Vineyard Community Church. I'm returning your call. Julia Scott-Norton told me that I'd be hearing from you. I'm so sorry to hear about the loss of your mother. How can I help you?"

"Perhaps I could come over to the church, and we could talk. I have to come down island later today to meet with her lawyer. Estate and probate stuff. "

"Down island?"

The man laughed. "It's an island thing. I'll explain when I get there. Could I come by at around three this afternoon?"

"Three is fine, Mr. Parker."

"Fine, I'll see you then. And call me Dan. We're pretty informal here."

When she hung up she looked at her watch. There was time. Maybe when she finished her coffee she should go over to Dory's house and have another look at that stair tread for herself before she said anything to anybody. But before she had time to wipe the second cappuccino mustache off her face, the telephone rang again.

"Madame Reverend?"

"This is Olympia Brown. Who is calling, please?"

"Sorry, Olympia. Wisecracking keeps me sane. It's Jack Winters. I'd like to come by with my sister. She'd like to meet you."

"Sure, what time?"

Actually, why don't we take you to lunch at the down-dog? Janney's playing golf, so it would just be the three of us."

"Down-dog?"

This time it was Jack who laughed at her ignorance of the island vocabulary.

"Black Dog Tavern. It's right on the water. The view and the food are great. Besides, you can't come to Martha's Vineyard and not go there at least once. I might even get you a tee shirt just to prove it. How about Melody and I pick you up at the church at noon?"

"That'll work. I don't have to be back at the church until three."

"No probs. We'll deliver you back at the appointed hour."

So much for my little investigative sojourn next door.

She looked at the clock. It was ten minutes after eleven. Between now and lunch there was just enough time to come up with a sermon title. After several minutes of wandering around in a mental and theological vacuum, she remembered something she'd read in Miss Winslow's diary. When Leanna Faith needed guidance, she took out her *Bible*, let it fall open to wherever it would and selected a random verse from the page open before her.

While Olympia would never consider herself a biblical scholar, she had, in fact, read it in its entirety and had always loved its enduring message and the sound of the elegant poetic language. She looked around the office for a *Bible* and found three on the bookcase under the window. She selected a dusty King James Version to begin her quest. The King James was not the most popular translation in use these days, especially among liberal scholars and theologians, but she stuck with it because of the beauty of the words. She set it on her desk and let it fall open into her two hands. Then, shutting her eyes like a child at a birthday party playing pin the tail on the donkey, she ran her index finger down the page on her right and stopped somewhere near the bottom.

"Woe unto them that call evil good and good evil; that put darkness for light and light for darkness; that put bitter for sweet and sweet for bitter!" Isaiah 5:20

Olympia felt something brush her shoulder. She jumped and whirled around in her chair, causing the *Bible* to fall to the floor with a crash. The office was empty.

Unsettled, she picked up the *Bible*, marked the chapter and verse, and set it out on her desk for when she returned from lunch.

~

The Black Dog Tavern was about as charming and folksy as anything Olympia could imagine. It was totally without pretense—or else carefully constructed to appear that way. The wide, well-worn floor boards creaked when she walked on them; the view of the harbor was indeed panoramic; and the food, when it was later presented, was delicious. As she, Jack Winters and his sister Melody made their way to a table by the window, a pale but steady Jack was greeted by over half the people in the place.

"Popular with the locals, then?" asked Olympia as she slid along the plank bench to her place.

"Popular with the year-rounders in the off season. Mostly tourists now, but if the locals get here early, we can usually get a seat." Jack took his napkin from beside the plate and smoothed it onto his lap. "I suppose I'm both. We have a house in West Tiz, but in the summer we mostly stay on the boat."

"West Tiz?" said Olympia.

"West Tisbury," said Melody. "It's an island thing."

The three made small talk while they perused the menu, decided upon their choices and waited for their meals. It was only later, over coffee and a huge slab of dangerously chocolate cake, that Jack began to talk about his health.

"They went in, had a look around with a little lighted thingamajiggy and found some serious stuff."

"Serious but not without hope," said his sister.

"Tell me more," said Olympia, setting down her fork and leaning forward.

Jack was twisting a drinking straw in his fingers. "Basically I need the whole nine yards, surgery, chemo, and radiation. It won't be pretty or fun, but if I do it all, I've got least a fifty percent chance for a few more good years. I've always enjoyed playing the long shots. Why should I stop now?"

Olympia said nothing but looked across the table at Jack's sister.

"We're going to have another consultation later in the week, but he should get started as soon as possible for the best results. I'm going to see if I can get a personal leave and come out here when he has the surgery and when he first comes home. I have responsibilities out there that I just can't walk out on."

"I can help," said Olympia.

Melody smiled. "You have responsibilities yourself, Reverend. Say a prayer, and be there for him and Janney. When we know more ourselves, I'll know what he and we all will need."

"So, I'm bad but not dead … yet," said Jack.

"Shut up and eat your cake, big brother. I may be five minutes younger than you, but I'm still the boss. You always were a contrary pain in the … I mean …" said his sister, turning as red as her hair.

Olympia giggled, waved away the embarrassment and tucked into the fragrant mountain of moist chocolate cake topped with melting vanilla ice cream. "When in doubt, eat," her mother had always said, and Olympia always agreed with her mother, at least when it came to matters of food.

Nineteen

At fifteen minutes after three, Daniel Parker stepped into her office, tapped his watch and said, "Seems I operate on island time."

"I heard it called black folks' time when I was in college. Then my priest friend, Jim Sawicki called it Polish time. Either way, I'm glad you're here. Do sit down." Olympia gestured to a small wooden armchair to the left of the door, and Daniel Parker moved it closer to the desk before he sat down. He wasted no words.

"My mother, Mary Parker, was very clear about not wanting a church service. She wanted to have only a few words said at the grave site, family only, and then have her ashes buried next to my father. After that, she wanted a big party at the P.A. club with everyone invited. My mother enjoyed a number of things, but being center of attention in a crowd of people was very high on the list."

"Tell me about your mother, Mr. Parker."

"It's Dan. My mother was a bright, able woman. She was generous, funny and demanding as hell ... and for her age, she was amazingly fit. She liked having things her way and usually found a way to make that happen. So it's no surprise that she made her final wishes so abundantly clear. What is a surprise is that she died falling down the stairs."

Dan Parker blinked his eyes a few times, then finally took out a handkerchief and wiped his eyes. "Sorry about this. It's just that she wasn't ready to go. She was a tough bird, my mother. Pain in the behind sometimes, but she was terrific. It doesn't make sense."

Olympia cocked her head to one side. "What doesn't make sense, Dan?"

"My mother falling down the stairs. She was OK on stairs, she always held the railing. I warned her about that. She didn't take chances."

"What exactly happened?"

"I'm not sure, but she must have been going downstairs with the laundry. The machines were in the basement. We were talking about having them moved upstairs, but she maintained that's how she got her exercise." He shook his head and dabbed at his eyes. "I should have insisted.

"Anyway, the day she fell, she must have started down and tripped or caught her foot or slipped on something. She must have grabbed for the railing and missed. That was it. Bang! Gone. The medical examiner said she was probably killed instantly."

"It wasn't a massive heart attack or a stroke, was it?"

"We're still waiting for the results of the autopsy. What tears me up is that she was there on the floor for a couple of days before we found her."

"That's dreadful, Mr. ... uh, Dan. I'm so sorry."

"But that's not all."

"What do you mean?"

"I know I should have visited her more, but she was always so busy with everything she did that she rarely had time. And after my divorce and with the kids grown, it seemed that I had twice as much to do as before. Can you imagine having to make an appointment to see my own mother? How could I have known she'd gone and sold the house? That was an unpleasant surprise on top of all of this."

"What are you talking about?" Olympia's voice was sharper than she had intended.

"I don't know all of it yet. That's another thing I'm trying to understand and pick my way through. Right now, it looks like sometime in the last year she put everything into a limited family trust with a lifetime tenancy agreement. At least it sounded like that when she told me. Why in God's name would she do that? She had money, and she knew how to manage it. So do I, if anyone's asking—and if they do, it's none of their business. But this is a small island, and everybody pretty much knows who's got what. That was a long way around to saying that I don't need her money. I wanted the house, though. I grew up in it. But I wasn't in any rush. I just figured that one day it would come to me. Now I'm not so sure."

"What do you mean?"

"I'm still trying to put it all together, but I think that somehow, without her knowing it, my mother signed away the house. I mean, it's simply not like her. On the other hand, maybe she was a little more past it than I realized."

"Dan, this is going to sound a bit strange, but would you mind taking me up to see your mother's house?"

"Not at all, but what are you getting at? What good would that do?"

"Now I'm the one who's not sure, and for the time being, anyway, I need to keep my reasons to myself; but if you don't mind, I'd like to look at the stairs that she fell down."

Dan shook his head. "Well, as a matter of fact I was planning on going up there tomorrow morning. We can't do anything about the service until we get her body back and have it cremated, so I suppose we could talk about that on the way. But I don't understand, what good would looking at her house do?"

"Right now, it's best that I not go into that either, because I don't want to be quoted; but read between the lines, Mr. Parker. For the time being, may I ask that you keep this conversation and anything we might talk about tomorrow confidential?"

"Of course, Reverend. About tomorrow, shall I pick you up here?"

"That makes sense. Around ten?"

"I'll be here."

"Thank you, Mr. Parker."

"Dan?"

"Dan."

When he was gone and the door had closed behind him, Olympia reached for the phone and dialed a number she knew by heart.

"St. Bartholomew's."

"Is Father Jim available? This is Reverend Olympia Brown calling."

"He's out, Reverend Brown. May I have a number where he can reach you?"

Olympia recited her cell phone number and added, "Please tell him it's urgent."

She checked the time. It was well into the afternoon. Where had the day gone? With a dubious title taken from an ominous verse in the *Bible* as a starting point for her next sermon, there was nothing left to do but go home and get going on it, but she couldn't seem to get her mind off the inconsistencies and troublesome events of the last several days. She sat back and started counting them off on her fingers.

She had heard nothing from Julia or Dory or William Bateson. Those first three were related to Dory and what was going to happen to her and her house. Jack Winters and his cancer and his alcoholic wife and the shared tragedy of their lost son were an entirely different and totally convoluted set of issues, but they were very much related to the church that she currently pastored. She moved on to the fingers of her other hand: her daughter Laura and the coming baby, her future with Frederick, her professional future in ministry, and what else? Although it was some distance from where she was presently sitting, the house in Brookfield, Massachusetts had its own untold story and cast of characters. It, too, was part of her unfolding story.

Olympia shook her head, closed up the office, locked the door of the church and walked down the brick path to her borrowed car. As she got in, she looked back at the wood shingled chapel and smiled. The building was capped by an open bell tower, and it was perfectly framed by the branches of a stately New England maple tree on one side and a towering long-needle pine on the other. It really was about as quaint as it gets. But then she had a very dark and unsettling thought. When she was alone in her office at the far back of that darling little chapel, she was really alone. *What would happen if I fell down or had some kind of emergency? Who would hear me if I called for help?*

When she got home she set her papers on the table by the window and looked around the tiny cottage she called home. The cats greeted her enthusiastically, because she was the bringer of food, but something was different. What was it? The impatient animals distracted her from her unease with much ankle-twirling and kitty chatter. It was mostly related to their stomachs, but it was also partly because they really were happy to see her. It was only after she'd fed them that she spotted what it was that had alerted her. It was the antique clock, the one she'd brought with her from Brookfield that she believed had originally been owned by her house-ghost and Mayflower descendent, Miss Leanna Faith Winslow. It was lying face down on the braided rug in front of the book case where it had either fallen or been knocked off by one of the cats ... *because clocks don't jump!*

Olympia reached down, picked it up and checked to see if it was damaged. Everything seemed to be intact, which was really immaterial, because it never had worked, at least not since she had claimed ownership of it. But it did sometimes send her a signal when Miss Winslow was trying to get her attention. *Good grief, has that spectral busy-body actually followed me here? And if so, what the hell is she trying to tell me this time?*

She laughed out loud at the absurdity of it. Who would believe she had a traveling house-ghost who seemed to have appointed herself her personal advisor and protector? Well, actually, two people would: Father Jim, her best friend ever in the world, and more recently Frederick, the man who could very possibly be a permanent part of her future. But she stopped laughing when she looked at the clock a second time. The two filigreed hands pointed to ten minutes after eleven, the exact time that very morning when she had opened the *Bible* looking for a sermon title and found one she didn't like. *Trust Miss Winslow to make her opinions known, even from a distance.*

Olympia replaced the clock on the bookcase and reopened the *Bible*. She had two choices: ignore the ominous warning and find herself a new quote that would be easier to work with, or stay the course and meet the challenge head on. Olympia shook her head and answered her own question. She really only had one choice, and accepting the challenge might help her sort out some of the mysteries that seemed to be plaguing her itinerant ministry here on the island. *Maybe that's what Miss Winslow is trying to tell me.*

With that question settled in her mind, she addressed the larger curiosity of the dark forces that seemed quite literally to be coming out of the woodwork and what, if anything, she should do about them. That, in turn, involved contacting Jim as soon as she could and asking the dear man if he was up for a visit to an idyllic, sleepy little picture book island? *And what about Frederick? What's he going to think?* Two is company, and three is a crowd, especially in her shoebox of a cottage. Olympia took out her cell phone and speed-dialed Jim's number.

"Hi, Jim? This is Olympia. I think I may need your help down here. How soon can you get to the ferry terminal in Woods Hole?"

~

When she got back to her apartment in Somerville, Laura Wilstrom placed the teddy bear she had been cradling since she left her birth mother on one end of the blue plaid sofa and lowered herself somewhat awkwardly onto the other. After a few minutes of contemplative silence, she reached for the phone and dialed her adoptive mother.

"Mum? I know you're probably curious, so I called you the minute I got back. All in all, I'd say it went well."

"You know this is your business, dear. All I need to know is that you are OK, but I'd be lying if I said I wasn't curious. What's she like?"

"She was nervous, but I was, too. It was a little awkward at first. I do want to get to know her more, but I need to let this much settle before I do."

"What do you mean?" said her mother."

"She's not what I expected. I wanted to be angry, and I guess I was until I actually met her."

"What happened?"

"I felt sorry for her. We were both pretty emotional. I want to get the whole story. Maybe next time. She's a minister."

"You told me that."

"And I have two half-brothers."

"Oh."

"Mum?"

"Mmmm?" It was more of a sigh than a question.

"You're my mother, and you always will be. You wiped my nose and gave me a great life until I went and messed it up. I did that all by myself. You had nothing to do with it."

"You didn't mess up your life, Laura. You made a decision that had unforeseen consequences. He seemed like such a nice man in the beginning. The important thing is, you're going to have a baby, and your dad and I are going to be grandparents. That trumps everything. We'll support you however we can. This is one baby that's not going to be given up for adoption."

Olympia's daughter didn't bother to wipe away the tears that were running down her face and dripping off her chin.

"Thanks, Mum, you've always been there for me."

"I always will be."

"I know that."

"Mum, would you like to invite her over here sometime?"

"Of course, if you want to, but not just yet, OK?"

"One step at a time, didn't you always tell me that?"

"I did," said her mother.

Twenty

William Bateson and the rest of the people that made up The Gingerbread Men were once again gathered in the back office of the pink and blue cottage that both fronted and disguised their operation. They were seated, each with a glass of something cold on the table in front of them, reviewing the details of the West situation. Because of the summer heat, a rusty air conditioner wedged into the single window was wheezing and clanking almost continuously as it chilled the room and completely obliterated the voices of the men inside to anyone passing by.

William Bateson was speaking. "As far as I know, the daughter is coming this week. I haven't met her, so I don't know what to expect. I can only hope that because she's an artist type, she doesn't have too much of a business head. When the time is right I'll propose the idea of putting the house in a protective trust so that she doesn't have to worry about it, and her mother is safe."

"What's not to like about that?" said Mary Beth Lessing, lawyer and legal consultant to the group. "That's when I usually come in with all the answers."

"They don't call us confidence men for nothing," said Mike Barnes, punctuating the statement with a laugh that sounded like someone choking.

"What about the Parker deal? Everything OK on that one? Nobody questioning the will?" Al Francis was drumming his fingers on the table, much to the evident irritation of William Bateson.

Mary Beth shook her head. "So far, so good, but she went to the same church as Mrs. West. That could be awkward if we're not careful. We didn't know that until recently. She never went to services. We don't want anyone getting curious. I had everything signed and notarized when Mrs. Parker started talking about calling her son, saying maybe she should take it back and have him look it over. But then the poor dear fell down the stairs."

"Accidents happen."

"Don't they just," said Al Francis. "We've never actually killed anyone before. That's not part of the plan."

It was an accident, do I have to spell it? It wasn't our fault the fall killed her. She fell wrong. Maybe she had a heart attack. Who knows."

"But ..."

"Get over it, Al."

Mary Beth spoke slowly and pedantically. "That's why, if we are going to continue with the West deal, we have to be really careful. We can't have any similarities, nothing that would raise a flicker of interest anywhere. This one could be a little too close for comfort."

Al Francis looked at the people seated at the table. "It is too close for me. Maybe we should cut bait and get out. We've got the Parker money, or we will have. People make mistakes when they get greedy, and we can't afford mistakes."

"Will you just chill? This one's too good to pass up. The place is a gold mine. With a little work we could double, if not triple, what I'm going to propose in the settlement. We're looking at two to three million between the house, land and her investments." William Bateson held out his hands, palms up towards his colleagues. "Trust me gentlemen, I'm a professional. The only thing that could really screw things up is if minister-lady gets too nosy, and I've already started working on that one."

"What do you mean?" asked Al.

"I mean, I seem to remember someone right in this room saying that accidents happen."

~

When he got back to the house in Brookfield, Frederick unpacked his overnight bag and opened every window in the old farmhouse that he could lift. Then he filled the largest drinking glass he could find with cold water and melted onto a chair at the kitchen table. The house was an oven. No matter how many times Olympia had assured him that it was safe to leave windows open when they were out, nothing in his urban English background would allow him to do it. It was not the way he did things, and now he was paying the price. Even the seat of the chair was hot.

He thought back on his all too brief visit with the woman he loved and then to the endless expanse of time before he would be seeing her again. Four whole days. Then, when an involuntary response to his amorous anticipation began to manifest itself, Frederick considered the twofold benefits of a cold shower. With no cats to feed and the heat of the day such that work in the garden was impossible, and work on his inside project, insulating the attic, would be downright suicidal, Frederick the lonely closed his eyes, thought of England and staggered off in search of a towel and a bar of soap. This was no way to spend a summer.

~

"Julia?"

"Mmmm, yes, Dory, what's on your mind? Would you like something cool to drink? I can't believe how hot it is today, and the humidity is making it even worse. It doesn't usually get this bad until August."

The two women were seated in the shade of the covered porch, hoping to catch a breeze off the water.

"No, thank you, dear, I can get it myself if I really want some. I was just thinking."

"Thinking about what?"

"I was thinking that maybe it really is time for me to move. I'm getting too old for this. I was thinking about those apartments for people like me, you know, the ones on the water in Vineyard Haven? I can't remember the name right now."

"Seacrest?"

"That's it. Maybe I should go down there and put my name on the list."

Julia Scott-Norton stopped fanning herself with the newspaper.

"Dory, promise me you won't do anything or sign anything or put your name on anything until your daughter gets here, OK?"

"I'm getting tired, Julia. I never thought I'd hear myself say that. But I suppose you're right, I need to wait at least until Jessica gets here. She's coming tomorrow, isn't she? Isn't that what I said?"

~

Jim leaned back in his reading chair and stared out of the window. His bedroom at St. Bartholomew's rectory offered a distant view of Dorchester Bay, and it never failed to soothe and help him think. *What in the world is she getting herself into this time?*

There was no doubt that the Reverend Doctor Olympia Brown, his beloved and most trusted friend in the world, had a nose for trouble. Beyond that, she had the very predictable habit of dragging him in on it because she knew she could depend on him to help, and she was right. But one of these days he feared that she was going to dig herself into a ditch that she couldn't get back out of, and then what? She had never yet let her head get in the way of her heart, and at fifty-something he didn't suppose she was going to start now. He shook his head and opened his calendar. It was midsummer, and miracle of miracles, he actually had a few clear days. He could take the two o'clock bus out of South Station and be at her place by five at the latest. *Piece of cake!*

Speaking of cake, he'd heard there were some pretty good restaurants on Martha's Vineyard. Maybe he would treat his friend to a nice meal in exchange for sharing a lumpy pull-out sofa with her two cats.

But something unspoken was flashing danger, something hovering out there beyond the fancy restaurant and the bottle of wine. Olympia was in a new situation, far from home and him and from Frederick, as well. For a woman who had done so much with her life, she could be hopelessly naïve when it came to people with devious intentions. He never wanted to pierce her bubble of optimism and generosity. It was one of the reasons he cared so much about her, but somebody needed to strike the reality gong now and then. *And Frederick, nice as he is, is too new to the American scene and too courteously, Englishly unassertive, to do it himself.*

Jim closed his eyes and rubbed his chin, his pondering position. This could be the opportunity he had been looking for, and trust God to hand it to him. There was something he needed help with that only a friend like Olympia would understand and not pass judgment on. He reached into his pocket for his pencil and started listing what he would need to take with him.

~

The meeting with the insurance adjuster was set for four that afternoon. At precisely ten minutes after the hour, Mike Barnes, Olympia Brown and Julia Scott-Norton were seated in Dory's living room along with Dory herself and her daughter Jessica. The famous cellist was wearing cut-off jeans, a green tank top and a harried expression.

Mercifully, after a terrifying thunderstorm in which Olympia's two cats actually spat and hissed at the door and then raced for cover, the weather had cooled down and dried out. But the change in barometric pressure didn't do much for the interior, contents and ambience of Dory West's soggy house. Because of the heat, the stench of the rapidly proliferating mold was almost overpowering. Julia wisely thought to bring a fan, and

Olympia followed suit and dragged one over from next door. Now seated together and yelling over the noise of the fans, they were trying to make sense of what the insurance adjuster, Mike Barnes, was telling them.

Olympia was doing her best to listen and take notes, but a piece of her outward professional demeanor was simply star struck. There was no other way to put it. She was sitting next to one of the most famous cellists in the world, Jessica West. Olympia had seen her in performance, but in real life, sitting in her devastated childhood home, she looked and talked just like any other daughter concerned for her mother's safety and well being. She tried not to stare. Jessica's skin was a shade darker than her mother's. She had green eyes, and her hair curled in tight, dark copper ringlets that framed her face. She had an angular body, and draped into the wicker rocker across from her mother, she looked like a long, graceful cat, relaxed but totally aware of what was going on around her and ready to spring if necessary.

The insurance adjuster was speaking. "I don't think you are going to like what I have to say, Mrs. West. The house is old and very much in need of repair, but at the same time, the flood damage is not enough to call it a total loss. Trouble is, you can't live in it until it's fixed, and it's going to take a lot of fixing. I'll do the best I can, but I can tell you right now the settlement will not cover what needs to be done.

Jessica straightened up in her chair and leaned forward. "So what is she supposed to do until then?"

"My personal and candid advice to both of you is to sell the place for whatever you can get and let someone else worry about fixing it. You take the money and move your mother into something that's easier for her to maintain."

Dory sat on the sofa with her eyes fixed on the floor, slowly shaking her head back and forth.

"Mum?"

Dory raised her head and then stuck out her little brown chin. "It's much too much to think about. I wouldn't even know where to begin, and thank you very much, Mr. Barnes, but I'm not going to start now. You can leave your estimates with my daughter, and we'll get back to you in a few days. My father used to say, 'this is gonna take some hard thinkin'… and after that a little bit of prayin'.'"

"Perhaps if I sent …"

Julia Scott-Norton stood up the way she did when she wanted to signal the end of a church meeting.

"You've been very helpful, Mr. Barnes. I think we understand each other. Dory has a lovely place to stay for as long as she needs it. She has her own bathroom and even a microwave and mini-fridge in her room. We need time to think about this from every angle, and that's exactly what we are going to do. We don't rush things on Martha's Vineyard."

No one got past Julia Scott-Norton when she signaled the end of something, and this was no exception. It was clear that Mike Barnes got the message. He made a great show of collecting his papers and putting them in order. Then, after giving a folder containing his findings and estimates to Jessica, he nodded farewell to the assembled ladies. Julia wasted no time in shutting the door firmly behind him and suggesting that the four of them continue their discussion next door in Olympia's cottage where the air was a little better.

It was a tight squeeze inside Olympia's one-person living room, but once they were all inside and had pulled chairs out of various corners, there was just enough room to seat them all. Julia did a quick recap of what had just transpired and suggested to Jessica that they would do well to get a second opinion. Jessica agreed that it was a good idea but added that she'd been concerned for some time about her mother living alone in such a big house — well, big for her. Managing it all while on concert tour was not easy, so maybe selling and moving was not such a bad idea, or maybe finding someone to come and live with her. It certainly would be easier for all concerned. Dory looked around at the women in the room. She was outnumbered by people who loved her.

"I have no idea what the house is worth," she said.

"That's easily found out," said Julia.

"William Bateson is a realtor. He's told me more than once if I ever wanted to sell, that he would help me. Why don't we call …"

"Let's get a second opinion on that as well," said Julia, interrupting and diverting her. "I think it's a good idea to get two or three estimates and then come to an agreement. But we might be getting ahead of ourselves. Dory, you and Jessica need to look at what Mr. Barnes has given to you and talk it over between yourselves. When you have come to a decision, that's when we can help, can't we, Olympia?"

Olympia had no choice but to agree. She cast a furtive glance at the wall clock in the kitchen. Jim had called and said he'd be on the five o'clock ferry out of Woods Hole. It would be docking in Vineyard Haven at quarter to six. That meant she needed to get over there in time to find a place to park, and she knew all too well that traffic at that time of the day was going to be vicious. This idyllic little island had more than one dark side, and Olympia wondered how many more she would uncover before her eight weeks were up.

Julia rose to her full, elegant height and said, "Well, ladies, I think we have done what we came to do. We have information and options. Jessica, why don't you and Dory join me for dinner? Olympia, you'd be most welcome to join us."

"Thank you, Julia, but I need to pick up a friend at the ferry at five forty-five."

Julia raised an eyebrow and cocked her head.

"It's a priest friend of mine. Actually, he's my best friend. He's coming down for a few days."

Julia looked around the tiny cottage with the question mark still arched in her eyebrow.

"She has a guest room," said Dory. It's about as big as an airmail stamp, but there's room enough for a single bed and a pair of shoes. Right, Olympia? I picked out the paint and the quilt myself."

Now it was Dory's turn to stand. "Dinner sounds lovely, Julia, but let's go out to a restaurant, and it will be my treat. You have been so kind. Your house embraces anyone who walks in the door. I need a way to say thank you for all you've done for me and my daughter." Dory turned to Olympia. "Why, we even have our own rooms."

Julia smiled and nodded. "I'd like to think I planned it that way, but the truth is, my mother and grandmother before me welcomed friend and stranger. I guess I inherited it."

"You are an absolute treasure," said Olympia.

"Tell my husband," said Julia.

Twenty-One

May 7, 1861

One week ago today, I returned to Brookfield with my son. And on that first Sunday, I carried him (more bravely than proudly perhaps) past the raised eyebrows and the questioning looks to my accustomed seat in our little village church. Should anyone have the temerity to ask, I say only that he has come to me by virtue (virtue indeed?) of another's folly. I said it was someone on my aunt's side of the family who could not keep him and didn't want him to go to a stranger. In promising to keep him safe, I promised to keep safe the mother's sorrowful secret and raise the child as my own. Let the busybodies pick the bones out of that! In the end, they will believe what they want.

Meanwhile, there is a garden to tend, a child to nurse, and a stray kitten the color of cooked squash who has decided that my little boy needs a companion. If the weather holds, I can put in the last of my seeds. Simple, ordinary tasks take so much more time these days.

More anon, LFW

~

The ferry arrived on schedule, and within minutes of its gliding along the dock and tying up, Jim, in a short-sleeved, pale yellow summer shirt and no clerical collar, waving his sunglasses on high, was striding down the metal walkway. The two embraced theatrically, and Olympia towed him off to her venerable Volvo.

"Hey, there, Vicar, that the gentleman friend we've not been privileged to meet as of yet, or do you have an island secret?"

Olympia didn't have to look up to know who it was. "Jack, meet Father James Sawicki. He's a dear friend and respected colleague. We've worked together for years. Now what was that you were saying?"

Jack coughed and sputtered, trying to pry his foot out of his mouth while Olympia and Jim stood by and snickered. Finally Olympia took pity on the man and intervened.

"Relax, Jack. He is a priest, but he is not wearing his collar because he's on vacation. If you are very nice to him, I might allow you to pour him a drink. But I warn you, he's a wine expert. He's got a very educated palate, and you, I remember, have a very fine selection of wines on that dandy little boat of yours."

"Oh, Christ, I mean crap … I mean …"

By this time Olympia and Jim were laughing so hard they had to hang on to each other to keep from collapsing. When she could breathe, she turned to Jim and said, "It's a small island, and you've just stepped off the boat. By tomorrow half the island will know I've got a house guest, and the other half will have invited you to dinner. Welcome to my new world."

"And let me be the first. Olympia, Jim, may I invite you both to my place on the water tonight for drinks and who knows what. My sister Melody is still here, and she'd love to see you again, Olympia. Whaddya say?"

"Sure," said Olympia, answering for the two of them. "Give me a couple of hours to show the man to his cubicle and let him put his feet up for a little bit after the commute, and we'd be delighted."

"OK, how about seven? That give you enough time?"

"Perfect," said Olympia.

Once they were under way and heading home, Jim turned to Olympia and said, "Is it like this all the time?'

"I don't know. I arrived after the start of the tourist season, so I don't know anything else. I do know there's a huge clear-out after Labor Day and a lesser one after Columbus Day. I understand that in the winter months this place is totally different. I think I could really like it then. It's nice, but I never have been one for crowds. That part is pretty overwhelming."

"You sound as if you don't like it now."

"No, I didn't mean to imply that. It's different. And it's nice, but that's not why I called you. I'll tell you everything once I get a glass of something cold into your hand. You'll want to save your taste buds for Jack's wine; he serves some pretty elegant stuff."

Jim leaned back and smiled. It was clear to Olympia that he was tired.

"You up for going out tonight?"

"I'll probably need a quick nap, but I'll be fine. I'm getting better at pacing myself."

"Since when did you need to pace yourself?"

"It's one of the things I want to talk about when we get back to the house."

~

As he approached the *Janney-Lee*, Jack Winters waved an energetic greeting to his two favorite women. Melody and his wife were sitting topside, each holding up an umbrella drink and picking at something colorful on a plate between them.

"We got some sushi. There's more downstairs if you want some."

"No, thanks. I bumped into The Reverend just now, and I invited her over for drinks later on. She's got a priest friend staying with her for a couple of days. 'Course, I didn't know he was a priest when she introduced me, so I kinda …"

"Blew it?" said his wife.

"You might say that, as well, but I confessed, and he forgave me."

"Bullshit," said his wife.

"You might say that."

Jack swung himself on board and joined the two women.

"How are you feeling?"

"No different than when I left two hours ago, Mel. That's the screwy part. I don't feel any different. Maybe that's a good thing. Ya think?"

Melody half-smiled at her brother. "That's the worst part of all of this is that people often don't feel anything other than maybe a little tired, or they start losing weight. Usually that's what sends them to the doctor."

"I guess it was both for me. But tomorrow we go back in, and I get the full report and the schedule for what happens next."

He was interrupted by the sound of breaking glass. Janney had dropped her drink and was looking confused.

Melody jumped up and grabbed a towel, and Janney threw up her hands. She looked both embarrassed and defeated. "Just shows what happens when I don't drink. Guess I'm not used to it. Maybe I'll have something when the holy orders arrive. On the other hand, maybe I won't."

"I'm not counting," said her husband.

~

As Olympia pulled up and parked in front of her cottage, she saw William Bateson coming out of Dory's house. When he caught sight of her he waved and rushed over to open her door and help her up onto the sidewalk.

"I was just looking for Dory; do you know where she is?"

"I'm not sure, William. Earlier this afternoon she was here with the insurance adjuster, and then she and her daughter Jessica both left with Julia Scott-Norton."

"They didn't say where they were going, did they? I need to ask Mrs. West something about the house."

Olympia sidestepped William and the question and opened the passenger door.

"William Bateson, meet Father Jim Sawicki, my best friend. He's a colleague of mine from another life."

Bateson held out his hand, and Jim shook it.

"To answer your question, when they left I heard mention of dinner at a restaurant somewhere, but I have no idea which one or what was on the schedule after that."

"Is she still staying with Julia?"

"Her daughter arrived this morning."

"Where is Dory staying, Reverend?"

"As far as I know, she's still with Julia. Maybe if you called over there."

"Well, if you see either of them before I do, would you tell her that I've got some numbers for Mrs. West?"

"I'd be happy to, but if you'll excuse us, Jim's been traveling most of the day, and he needs to freshen up."

William stepped back and inclined his head. "Of course. Nice meeting you, Jim. I hope our paths will cross again when we've got more time. I love to hear news from the outside world."

"Oh, it can't be that bad down here," said Jim, looking around.

"Yes, it is," said Olympia and William Bateson simultaneously.

The first words out of Jim's mouth when he was behind a closed door were, "I don't like that guy."

"He's one of the reasons I asked you to come down here."

"One of the reasons, you mean there are more?"

"How long have you got?"

"I hate it when you say that. It always means you are up to your neck in alligators, and you've forgotten how to drain the swamp … again."

"Let's just say he's just one of the alligators. Look, I don't need to be a rocket scientist to figure that you need a rest. We can talk when we get back tonight. The shoebox just off the kitchen is yours. I measured it. The room is eight by six, exactly enough room for a single bed. There are some pegs on the wall beside the door for your clothes and a towel. It does, however, have a window that opens, and the cats don't go in there."

Jim didn't need a second invitation, and within a few minutes Olympia learned that Jim snored. *Sounds just like one of the cats purring*, she thought and then smiled. Her friend was there. Whatever was going on and whatever might happen next didn't feel so threatening now. Olympia scooped up Thunderfoot, the larger and younger of the two cats, and sat down in her chair. Soon they too were ... purring.

When Jim surfaced, he had a quick shower, and the two of them made ready for a social evening aboard the *Janney-Lee*. On the drive to Oak Bluffs Harbor, Olympia pointed out spots of interest and promised Jim a walking tour of the famous campground along with an ice cream cone as big as his head.

"Is this a bribe?" he asked, trying to look in all directions at once.

"Not at all, Jim. This place really is beautiful, charming and unlike anything else you'll ever experience. I want to share it with you."

"And you like ice cream."

"You know me too well, my friend, but it really is like walking around inside a storybook."

"With some very dark chapters."

"That's why I asked you to come down. Oh, look, we're here, and would you believe it, there's even a parking spot. There is a God somewhere, and tonight she's on my side."

Jim crossed himself and groaned.

Later that evening when they were back in Olympia's cottage and they could speak freely, she filled him in on the series of troubling events thus far and the attendant unanswered questions surrounding them. Even she had to admit that in just over a week of her being on the island, it was quite a list.

Jim looked at his best friend and shook his head. "What is it with you? Are you some kind of trouble magnet? Every time I turn around, you're tangled up in something that needs more than passing attention, and then you call me to bail you out."

Olympia leaned back in her chair and held up her hands, palms out in the not-me position. "The only person I'm really concerned about in all of this is Dory, and quite frankly, it's the only situation I might be able to do something about. Jack Winters and family need pastoral support. That's clear, and I can do it. But Dory may or may not be the target of a person or persons intending to con her out of her property. That's where I may be in over my head."

"So what can I do?"

"I'm not sure yet, Jim. Once I get wind of something, the first stage of my amateur investigations involves collecting information, which I'm still doing. The next step is talking it over with you—and Frederick, when he's around."

"So where is your hopeful, helpful Englishman? I was hoping he'd be here."

"Back in Brookfield, tending hearth and garden. He was here over the weekend."

"And you didn't talk it over with him?"

"There wasn't really anything to say. It's only recently turned suspicious, and even now it still could all be circumstantial, and I'm the one that's blowing it out of proportion."

Jim leaned back on the sofa. "Start at the beginning, Olympia."

And that's exactly what she did. It was well after midnight when she finished, and the two were slit-eyed and yawning. The cats had already gone to bed.

"Let me sleep on all of this, Olympia. What's on for tomorrow?"

"That's part two of the developing drama."

"What the hell are you talking about?"

"An elderly parishioner died in an accidental fall just before I got here. Unfortunately, I'm finding some unpleasant parallels to that situation and what's going on right now with Mrs. West. Tomorrow morning, the woman's son, Dan Parker, is taking me to her house so I can see where it happened."

"Has he any idea of what you're thinking?"

"Let's just say we both have some unanswered questions. I didn't want to say too much to him at this stage, but there's a real estate-slash-legal issue in this one, as well."

"Good thinking. Want me to come along?"

"Thanks, Jim, and no thanks, but trust me. If I think a second visit or a clerical consultation is in order, you'll be the first to know. Meanwhile, the Rev. Doc prescribes a lazy morning, maybe a gentle walk along the water and some serious cat-patting. I won't be gone long."

Twenty-Two

Outside the front of the church Dan Parker eased up on the clutch of the faded maroon Mercedes and slipped into the crawl of summer traffic inching along Main Street.

"You can roll down the window if you're too hot. This car was made before air conditioning was standard equipment. It's my island car — old, ugly and dependable."

Olympia cranked open the window as instructed and let the humid sea breeze do its worst on her already limp, gray-streaked hair. She'd given up on high maintenance hair years ago and made do with a wash and wear style that she cut herself. As she pushed a vagrant strand out of her eyes, she remembered her sons when they were in grade school, begging her to go to a salon and have a real haircut and think of having it frosted or streaked so maybe she wouldn't look so much like, well, somebody's mother. Olympia smiled at the memory and then brought herself back to the present.

"I never thought to ask, but does your ex-wife have any thoughts about all of this? Are you still in contact with her?"

"We've been divorced for years. I don't even know where she's living right now. My mother never liked her."

"I'm sorry. I either shouldn't have asked or asked more delicately."

"Believe me, it's not an issue. It was a long time ago, but I might as well finish the picture. I think I mentioned that I have grown kids, a son and a daughter, both living on their own. I get along pretty well with them, but they've got their lives, and I've got mine."

"You never married again?"

"Never saw the need. I don't know, maybe someday." Dan shrugged his shoulders and stared at the road ahead.

Time to change the subject!

"Ummm, how long do you think this humidity going to last?"

"Thanksgiving?"

Olympia made a face, then pulled a wadded piece of paper towel out of her pocket and wiped her forehead. "Certainly drains the energy."

The two continued to make small talk about the weather, the state of the world economy, the influx of Brazilian workers over the summer and how cruelly they could be exploited, and nothing about the circumstances of his mother's death. When they arrived at the up-island home of the late Mary Elgin Parker, a sun-bleached, grey-shingled sprawl of indeterminate age, Dan sighed and started up the bumpy dirt road to the front door. The house was set well back from the street and surrounded by acres of rolling grassy hills, sparse scraggy oaks, and all of it demarked by irregular stone walls. It was breathtaking. Olympia could easily see why no one in his or her right mind would ever want to part with it—and why someone else might find it so very desirable. *But to what ends would a person go to get it?*

When they were inside Dan opened a few windows, got them each a glass of cold water, and directed Olympia to the chair with the best view of the distant silver sea.

Olympia sat and took a grateful sip of the water. With the windows open it was much cooler than down-island in Vineyard Haven.

"This is too lovely for words, Dan. I can see why it is so important that you keep it in the family, but that's not the point, is it? We want to know who or what made your mother change her mind. Tell me, have you learned anything more about the supposed sale?"

"Unfortunately, it's not supposed, it's a fact. I'm going to fight it, of course, but it's hard to get the energy with her so recently and suddenly gone. None of it makes any sense. This is so unlike her."

"Dan, can I ask you a few questions about all of this?"

"Isn't that what we're here for?"

Olympia shifted in her chair. "Let me get right to the point. I think there might be something suspicious going on. Your mother, a healthy, active woman in her early eighties, used to going up and down stairs, dies in an accidental fall."

"She'd still be playing tennis if I hadn't taken away her racket." Dan managed a weak smile, cleared his throat and wiped a speck of dust out of the corner of his eye. "Before she had ... the accident, unbeknownst to anyone in the family, she put the house and land into some kind of permanent trust with a lifetime tenancy. She was vague about the details, and I was too busy at the time to come running up here and check.

"Actually, now that I think about it, back around Christmas time she mentioned something about the house and a long term plan to keep it in the family. She said she had a new financial advisor who had recommended it. I think she said it was someone who gave a talk at one of the senior centers here on the island. As she understood it, she would have lifetime tenancy, and when she passed, the house would always be safe for the descendents. No one could ever get it out of the trust."

"So what did you say to her?"

"I told her not to do anything until I had a chance to talk to this person myself."

"And?"

"And I never got around to it. She didn't bring it up again, and I'm so busy with my business and my own life that I, well, I just didn't."

"Did your mother tell you the person's name?"

"No, but now that I think about it, she referred the advisor as 'her.' It was a woman. Of course, I don't have a name. I suppose it will be somewhere in her papers, but I looked in her desk, and I can't find them. That's another mystery, but I'll admit that I didn't look too carefully. Maybe she hid them or something, and that's not like her either. I just don't know what to think."

Olympia set her glass on a coaster on the coffee table. "Dan, hearing this, I'm even more convinced something very wrong is going on here. Can we go look at the place where she fell?"

"I guess I've been putting it off, but what are you talking about?"

"Remember yesterday when I asked that our conversations be held in confidence? Well, I'm underlining that now, OK?"

He nodded.

"I have reason to believe that something similar is happening with another member of the church. I'm not going to say who or exactly what right now, but there is another older lady with a valuable piece of property who I think may have been given a similar offer. She's also had an accident that is totally out of character for her. This one didn't kill her, but it wrecked the house. And the pencil on the staircase that I slipped on could have been dropped by accident or deliberately left there, but either way it could have resulted in a serious fall."

"Did you say you found a pencil on the stairs in that other house?" Dan was on full alert. "We found a screwdriver on the floor beside her body. Since there was no sign of any kind of struggle, the medical examiner figured she might have stepped on it and lost her footing. Her bruises were consistent with a fall. There was no other sign of foul play, but none of it makes sense. My mother doesn't use a screwdriver. She has a handy man that does odd jobs for her, that is, did her odd jobs."

"Do you know if he was there any time near the accident?"

"He was the first person I called. He hasn't been near the place since before Easter."

"Show me where she fell, Dan, and do you by any chance have the screwdriver?"

"It should be still there. I couldn't bring myself to touch it."

Dan opened the cellar door, turned on the light and led Olympia down the stairs. She could see an irregular red-brown stain on the cement floor, but she said nothing.

"This is where they found her." Dan dropped down onto the bottom step and covered his face with his hands. Olympia put a gentle hand on his shoulder and waited in silent witness to the man's grief.

"I'm so very sorry, Dan. This has to be awful."

He took out a handkerchief, blew his nose, and looked up at Olympia. "I swear to God, Olympia, if some son of a bitch killed my mother, I'm going to see him hang."

Or see her hang, thought Olympia. The mention of a woman in all of this changed and complicated the picture considerably, but it was not the time to mention that to the man sitting at her feet.

"Dan, you said that there was a screwdriver down here when they found your mother. Did you pick it up?"

"Actually, I remember seeing it and then kicking it across the room."

"Where did you kick it?"

"Just over th ..." He pointed in the direction of the washer and dryer and froze. "It's not there."

"Think now, Dan. You didn't pick it up or throw it out? You were very upset."

"No. I remember looking back at it as I went up the stairs after they took her away. I remember wanting to burn it or do something to damage it, but I left it there on the floor. I couldn't touch it."

"And it's not there now?"

"It's gone, Olympia."

On the way back to the church, Olympia told Dan everything that she knew about what was happening next door and everything she suspected, carefully mentioning only Dory's name and not that of William Bateson or any other members of the church who were involved. The flood at Dory's house had already been reported in both island newspapers, so she wasn't saying anything that was not already public knowledge. But the fact that someone had suggested that Dory put the house in trust with a lifetime tenancy was an unpleasant parallel that needed further investigation. Before she got out of the car, she reminded Dan of the need for confidentiality and asked if he would please contact her after he talked with his lawyer and let her know what he learned.

The thought of a woman involved in all of this was troubling Olympia. She didn't usually think of women as villains. Women were supposed to be the nurturers and the healers, not the destroyers; but that was stereotypical thinking, and she was unpleasantly surprised to catch herself doing it. Up until then, if there was something unhealthy going on, everything thus far pointed to William Bateson. So where was the truth? Dan's mother suffered a cruel accident, and there seemed be some similarities between that situation and what was happening with Dory West right now. *Are they connected? And how the hell am I going to find out?*

~

When she got back to her own house, Olympia made coffee and dragged Jim out onto her little deck where they could sit in the fresh air. Speaking in a low voice so as not to be overheard, she recounted everything that had happened that morning. To that she added her rapidly growing concerns about the house and the woman next door and the emerging and uncomfortable parallels to the Parker situation. When she finally ran out of steam and information, Jim suggested that she go and have a talk with Dory and her daughter and see if she could determine exactly how much pressure William Bateson was putting on Dory to sell and exactly what terms he was proposing.

"You might also check into Bateson's background and see what you can find out about him. Nowadays, it's easier and easier to find things like that on line."

Olympia shook her head. "I'm still at the bottom of the learning curve on that stuff, Jim. Remember, you're looking at someone who just learned how to answer her cell phone before it stops ringing. I can do e-mail, and I can write sermons on the computer, but beyond that it's still a struggle. I'm getting there, but ..."

"OK, let me do that. Besides, here in New England the fact that I'm a priest opens some doors and loosens some tongues that a lay person might not be able to manage."

Olympia shot him a menacing look.

"Look, girlfriend, don't go all feminist indignant on me. The truth is, like it or not, some people are still getting used to the idea of women clergy. You don't even wear a collar, so how would anyone know to give you special preference or attention?"

"Sometimes I do, wear a collar, that is."

Jim shook his head. "You're off the point, Olympia. Look, I'll do some computer research, and you find out what you can on foot, so to speak. Start with Mrs. West and her daughter. When I get back to Boston, I'll nose around the Boston police files and do a computer search on real estate scams and the elderly. It's entirely possible I might find something useful."

"Meanwhile, what about Mrs. Parker?"

"Why don't you call some of the local clergy and ask if they've run into anything like this in their churches? Clergy usually have a pretty effective underground network, and with this place being so small, they probably know some of the people involved."

"Now that you mention it, there's an Island Clergy Association meeting sometime this week. Deb, the church administrator, left me a note about it in my mailbox. But I don't really know any of them well enough to just call out of the blue and ask about a possible murder in one of their churches. See what I mean?"

Jim nodded. "OK, maybe not now, but if you get the chance. Meanwhile," he shut his eyes and wiggled his fingers in front of Olympia's eyes, "I am a fortune teller. You are going on a journey. You are sitting at a table. I see wine glasses."

Olympia laughed. "I guess you're hungry? All this amateur sleuthing makes me hungry, too."

"Anything makes you hungry, Olympia. What are you offering?"

"That you take me out to lunch at a restaurant I couldn't otherwise afford."

"Didn't I hear that the island was dry?"

"Edgartown and Oak Bluffs are wet, and both towns have some very nice restaurants. I'll drive."

"You know how to get there?"

Olympia harrumphed. "More important than knowing how to get there, Jim, I know which ones have parking. It's high season, and parking places are rare commodities." She made a face. "It's one of the downsides of the place they don't mention in the brochures. Just give me a minute to get my things."

Olympia checked the cats' food and water, ran a wet wash cloth over her face and neck, and announced she was ready.

"By the way, Jim. In all this kerfuffle over real estate deals and misdeals, house floods and shady characters, I haven't told you about the meeting with my daughter. But I'll save it for when I have the glass of elegant wine you are going to choose for me."

It was Jim's turn to make a face, but it was a fond smile in Olympia's direction.

"Lead the way, Reverend Doctor Brown."

Twenty-Three

June 19, 1861

I have a whole new respect for growing things these days. Both my garden and my son are flourishing, and between the two my days at home are most agreeably full. And once the townsfolk stopped wagging their heads and their tongues, many of the women came forth to offer advice and to admire little Jonathan. Already he is turning himself over and reaching for Sammy, the little orange tiger cat that will not leave his side. And yet despite all this great abundance, my heart is ever heavy with my secret. This darling child will never know the man who fathered him — nor I the fleeting love we only chanced upon. Alas, I cannot dwell upon such sorrowing. I'm told it will sour my milk.

But son and cat and garden, fulfilling as they be, will not be enough for me ere long. Before his birth I wanted to study for the ministry. That door is likely closed to me, at least for now ... but if not that, then what? My mind is restless and I long for more. It has ever been thus. My father used to say I should have been born a man. It is believed by many that women are only fit for a quiet domestic life inside the home. I repeat, I am restless and I long for more, and one day, I will find a way.

More anon, LFW

While Olympia and Jim were considering where to have their pricey lunch, Frederick was taking a break from number three on the list of house-tasks that he and Olympia had written out before she left for Martha's

Vineyard. This called for a beer. It was well after midday, and as far as he was concerned, in keeping with tradition, the English can drink any time. Frederick did draw the line at beer with cornflakes.

Today's task was replacing a loose tread on the narrow twisting staircase that led from the great room in the two-hundred-plus year antique house up to the second floor. The old tread lay on the kitchen table in front of him, and he was examining it as he savored his cold beer. The blanket of humidity that lay over the island where Olympia was currently living had extended itself over the water and up the coast to Brookfield. Frederick was trying to alleviate his discomfort with the contents of the can in his hand. He didn't like beer in cans. Beer belonged in glasses, and it was supposed to be room temperature; but he was in the States now, and mercifully, no one in the homeland of his dear Queen could see how far he had fallen.

He was hot, he was tired, and he was lonely. Not a good combination for concentration, but not even a hot, tired, lonely Englishman could fail to see the way an old but well-constructed stair tread should look and compare it to the stair tread that had come loose in Olympia's landlady's house. There was no doubt in his mind now that someone had worked it loose. *And that someone is on the island with my Olympia!*

"My Olympia?" he said aloud to the table before him and then slapped the table top with his fist for emphasis. He had brought his mother's engagement ring along with him to offer her as a token of his affection and, more specifically, as an invitation to become his wife. But every time he got even close to asking, she would switch gears and dodge the subject. That was about to change starting right now.

Frederick swallowed the last of his beer, tossed the can in the direction of the recycling box, and got up from where he was sitting. Despite his concerns and his desire for haste, he would delay long enough to have a shower and make himself a bit more presentable. Then he would put the box containing the ring in his pocket, climb into Olympia's van, and at what passed for breakneck speed, get himself to the ferry terminal at Woods Hole.

~

In Somerville Laura Wilstrom was sitting in a rocking chair, looking out the second floor window at the tree-lined street below. She was thinking about her two mothers. There was the one who had raised her and loved her enough to encourage her to try and locate her birth mother. And there was that other mother, the one she had planned to despise for abandoning her at birth, Olympia Brown, whom she had just met. She didn't despise her anymore and given time, she might even grow to like her, really like her. At first she had been nervous, but that was understandable, and once they both relaxed Olympia seemed nice enough. Laura was of two minds. With respect to the growing life within her, she needed to know her genetic heritage, and only one person could tell her this. *But can a daughter be loyal to two mothers? Can, or should, I try? And if I do, will I run the risk of hurting them both?*

There was no question in her mind that she would see Olympia again. She wanted to know more about her as a person, as another woman really, and know how she lived her life from the time she'd been born until now. Too, she needed to know more about her father. *I know I'm half Jewish, and he came from Oregon, and he went to Northeastern. That's a start.* But would there ever be any more than that?

At least Olympia had taken the first step in reconnecting with her. In their short time together Laura had already noted some similarities of gesture and speech inflection. So the real questions were, when would she see Olympia Brown again, and how much of what happened after that would or should she share with the mother who had raised her? Her curiosity about her birth mother was enormous, but her loyalty to her adoptive mother was even greater than that.

The children on the sidewalk below were playing jump rope and chanting the same sing-songs she had when she was a little girl, when life at home was cornflakes in the morning and peanut butter and jelly sandwiches for lunch, and homework had to be done before she could go out to play. Laura rested her two hands on her belly. As if on cue, the baby moved within her. She pressed her hands against the movement, and as she did, she wondered what kind of a world this child would come into. Motherhood and its incipient reality was beginning to take on a whole new dimension for Laura, Baby Girl (Faith) Brown, Wilstrom.

~

In his frantic determination not to miss the boat, Frederick took a running leap and made it over the two feet of water and onto the freight deck of the ferry as it began to pull out of the slip. He skidded to a stop to the cheers and applause of the crew and did his best to appear unfazed by brushing a bit of dust off the cuff of his shirt and checking his watch. He had left Olympia's car in the parking lot and taken the shuttle bus along with several vacationers who had boarded only moments before in peace and stately tranquility; but Frederick was 'bursting for a pee,' as he would later say, and damn near missed the boat because of the detour.

When he stopped hyperventilating and had collected what dignity he could salvage, he walked up the stairs to the snack bar on the top deck and ordered a cup of tea. No matter what the weather, the latest political scandal or the state of the world economy, "a nice cup of tea" is the Englishman's cure for everything from hemorrhoids to a broken heart. As he sat sipping the steaming liquid he thought about how and where he would corner Olympia to press his suit and give her the ring he'd prudently buttoned into his shirt pocket. Then he laughed at the ridiculous incongruity of it all. The last thing his darling Olympia would likely ever do was press a suit, his or anyone else's, and Frederick, wise fool that he was, already knew better than ever to suggest it.

~

William Bateson circled the block a second time to make sure Olympia's car was nowhere in sight before parking a block away and approaching Dory's empty house through the back yard of the house next door. He let himself in through the kitchen door and wrinkled his nose. The fetid smell of dampness and mold, enhanced by the overpowering humidity, was just what the doctor ordered.

The worse it looked and smelled, the better it was for making it look like a hopeless insurance case. He looked around the kitchen, remembering the day of the flood, and allowed himself a smile of satisfaction. It was all working out so well. All he had to do now was to wait until the daughter got the hell out of there, and they were home free. Still, it never hurt to keep up the pressure.

~

Dory West and her daughter Jessica were sitting with Julia Scott-Norton in the comfortable living room of Julia's West Chop home. The three were discussing the pros and cons of restoring Dory's house as opposed to declaring it a loss and moving Dory to a more manageable place, possibly nearer her daughter. Dory was adamant in wanting to restore the house and get back into it as soon as possible, while Julia was tactfully trying to point out the benefits of considering the possibilities of a smaller and more manageable home on Martha's Vineyard — or maybe even an independent living situation nearer her daughter.

Jessica, strategically seated between the two, was trying to help her mother see the advantages of all her options, but the thrust of her chin and the fact that she was leaning back in the wicker rocker with both her arms and her ankles crossed made it obvious that she was having none of it. Dory wanted one thing only and that was to go back home.

Julia tried a different tack.

"Dory, if you are determined to go back to your house, let's look at exactly what that's going to involve. You know you can stay here for as long as you want. I've got the room, and I truly enjoy your company; but it does mean that you will be here for at least four to six months. We simply cannot get a carpenter to do anything in the high season. You've lived here long enough to know that. So it will likely be after Christmas when you get moved back in, and that's being optimistic."

"You could come and stay with me for some of that time," offered Jessica, "but I'm away on tour a lot, so you'd be alone. So maybe that's not such a good idea."

Dory shook her head and turned toward Julia. "I don't know anyone in California. This is home, and this is where I belong." She uncrossed her arms and looked at Jessica. "If I could stay here for the summer, come September I can get a winter rental within walking distance of the house. That way, I'll be on my own and still be able to supervise the repairs."

Jessica rolled her eyes and shook her head. "OK, Mum, but let's not make any decisions until we get the final figures from the insurance adjuster. Then maybe we can get someone to come and look at the place and give us a rough estimate of what is going to be needed and how long it's going to take. I'd feel a whole lot better with some numbers and a time line before we go any further."

Dory re-crossed her arms. "Your father always said, 'there's nothing been broke that can't be fixed.' Well, girl, my house is broke, but I'm going to get it fixed, and that's that."

Julia, in her compassionate wisdom, moved into the impasse. "Dory, you just gave us the first plan of action. You'll stay with me for the summer, and we'll look into a winter rental in September. That will buy us some time to make the right decision, which I do believe we need more than anything else. Isn't that so, Jessica?"

Both Jessica and Dory nodded.

"There," said Julia, getting up off the sofa and stepping over the ever-present dog. "With the business at hand out of the way, I think we are in need of food and drink. Would anyone like a cup of tea?"

"I think I'd like a small glass of sherry," said Dory, uncrossing her arms and her ankles and reaching down to pat the dog.

"I'd like a large sherry," said Jessica, "and no ice."

~

William Bateson, Alden Francis, Mike Barnes, and Mary Beth Lessing, were seated around a table in the back office of Gingerbread Men Associates. Despite the best efforts of the window AC unit, the heat and debilitating humidity were affecting the patience and tempers of all present. William Bateson was speaking.

"I really thought the daughter was going to be the problem, but I'm getting the impression that she wants the old lady to sell. It's the minister that's turning out to be the sticking point. If we can get her to butt out, I think we're home free."

Mary Beth was fanning herself with a real estate magazine. "And how do you propose we accomplish that little detail? From what you've said, she's pretty tenacious."

"We can't afford to take any more foolish chances," said Al.

Bateson fired a dark look across the table.

"We're going to wait her out. How risky is that? She's only here for a couple more weeks, and then she's gone. Our trusty insurance adjuster here will drag his feet and cook the books while he's at it. Once the daughter goes back to wherever she goes back to, dear little Dory is ours for the plucking."

"We may not have that much time. Mary Parker's son Dan left me a message on my answering machine, says he has some questions about his mother's estate. Of course, I didn't return the call, but it's getting a little tight even for me."

"The West package is a big one," said Barnes. "Who here wants to pass on a deal worth between two and three million dollars when all we have to do is wait?"

"And if minister-lady doesn't go away?"

William Bateson ran a damp finger around the inside of his collar and looked sideways at the doubtful Al Francis.

"She'll go," he said.

~

Olympia turned the old Volvo into the parking lot behind the Harborview Hotel in Edgartown and, on top of that, managed to find a shady spot. The hotel restaurant was a favorite of many of her parishioners, and she was looking forward to trying it herself. They would have a nice meal, enjoy a fantastic view, and say what they needed to say without being overheard. After ordering a glass of expensive wine each, plus a gourmet salad with roasted vegetables and goat cheese for Olympia and a roast beef panini with horseradish cream for Jim, Olympia began with her most pressing story. She told him about Dory and the unclear questions surrounding the flood, the suspiciously loose stair tread, and the pressure on Dory to sell the house. Then she went over the questions surrounding the death of Dan Parker's mother and the suspicious parallels between that situation and what was happening with her landlady. She saw no need to tell him about Jack Winter's cancer but did speak briefly about the meeting with her own daughter. These last two were concerns of hers but nothing that Jim could affect.

What she needed was Jim's wisdom and point of view regarding real estate scams and elderly victims, which he agreed to research when he returned to Boston. He cautioned her to be careful about being too vocal or public about her concerns lest she tip her hand and put herself at risk. This last bit of advice was met with a dismissive wave of her hand and assurances that she wasn't stupid, nor was she born yesterday. At this last, Jim shrugged his shoulders and asked for the bill.

When they stepped outside on the hotel veranda, Olympia suggested they stroll out to the light house and look at the memory walk, a brick pathway engraved with the names of children who had died. Olympia plucked a pale pink beach rose from a bush growing along the path and placed it on the stone marked for Jack and Janney Winters' son Allan. After that the two friends sat in silence at the edge of the water and watched the On-time ferry shuttling back and forth across the harbor. Olympia was idly scooping up handfuls of warm sand and letting it slide through her fingers onto the tops of her bare feet.

Jim picked up a scallop shell and cleared his throat.

"I went to see my doctor last week. " He paused as if trying to find the words to continue. "I've been feeling tired and weak for the last couple of months, and I couldn't seem to shake it. She did a bunch of tests and then called me in and told me that my numbers are up."

Olympia dropped her sand and turned to her friend. "What do you mean, your numbers are up? What are you talking about?"

"My T-cells, Olympia. Although I've never actually said it, I suppose you figured out that I'm HIV positive?"

"Actually, I hadn't, but I'm not surprised to hear it. You told me that Paul died of AIDS, and you two were lovers."

"We were married, Olympia, in a Unitarian Church in Provincetown. One of your guys — a woman, actually — did the honors. Not legally, of course, but we had a ceremony. We even had a cake."

Olympia reached for Jim's hand. Despite the heat, his fingertips were cool to the touch.

"What are you telling me, Jim?"

"I'm saying that I might not be able to continue at St. Bart's, or at the very least, I might have to take a leave of absence for health reasons."

"Do they know? I mean the bishop or archbishop or whatever you call the head honcho around there."

Jim shook his head and looked away. "You know what would happen if I told them. No, they don't know, but I don't know how much longer I can hide it. I hate living a lie, Olympia, but I love being a priest. This is what I'm called to do, and if this gets out, I might not be able to continue. If I can't be a priest, I don't know what else I can do."

"You told me that when you met Paul, you left seminary and went into social work. But I think it's a little early to start thinking in that direction. What else did the doctor say?"

"To tell you the truth, I thought I'd dodged the bullet. I've been HIV positive for years, but I've been asymptomatic. I didn't need to go on any kind of a drug regimen. My HIV was nothing more than a notation in my medical records, and I pretty much stopped thinking about it, but it seems that my luck has run out. She told me she would put me on 'the cocktail,' as they call it, and the side effects may or may not be bothersome. If I take really good care of myself and follow doctor's orders, I should be able to continue working without too many problems."

"Did she give you any kind of a prognosis?"

"She couldn't or wouldn't say. Every case is different. Every person is different. Every person's response to the medication is different. She did say that because I was able to stay off the medication for as long as I have, that I could start with a minimal dose and monitor how I react. And because I'm physically fit and I don't smoke and I don't drink to excess, the prognosis should be encouraging. But come on, Olympia, how do you define encouraging?"

Olympia chose her words carefully.

"Did she actually tell you to take some time off?"

"She said it would help if I could cut back to part-time. I know I've been working too hard, but with the shortage of priests these days, all of us are working too hard. If I have to explain why I have to back off a little bit, I could get asked to leave."

"Can they actually do that?"

"They can do anything they want to, Olympia. I took a vow of obedience. As long as I'm a priest, I do what I'm told. My colleagues may have figured out that I'm gay, but it's not something we talk about. We both know that people can be very good at looking the other way if it suits the purpose. You know, don't ask what you don't want to know."

"That kind of thing happens everywhere, my friend, but even priests must get vacations. You could come and be here with me on Martha's Vineyard, or better yet, I can clear out another room in the Brookfield house. That way, you can come and go as you wish with no one in Rome or Boston any the wiser."

"Thanks, Olympia, that's very generous of you. I don't know what I'm going to do right now. It's too much to think about. Besides, not all of the test results are back."

"But the doctor does recommend taking some time off?"

Jim nodded.

"OK, then we need to come up with a reason for your doing so that isn't an outright falsehood but is close enough to the truth that it sounds plausible."

"Sounds like me trying to wangle a later curfew out of my mother when I first started to drive," said Jim.

Olympia grinned at her friend. "Some things never change."

"Oh, but they do ... but, shouldn't we be getting back before the whole island is talking about your sitting beside the Edgartown lighthouse holding hands with a strange man?"

"Let 'em!" said Olympia.

Twenty-Four

When Jim and Olympia returned to her purple and white cottage on West Maple Street, they were astounded to find Frederick sprawled in a wicker rocker on the front porch. There was a half-done crossword puzzle in his lap and a pencil lying across his upturned hand, and he was sleeping loudly.

Olympia didn't know whether to shriek in surprise, joy or dismay, so she did none of the above. She was delighted to see him, but her joy was tempered with the clear and present reality that trying to have any private time in such a small space with a house guest in the next room was going to demand some creative imagination.

"Well, here's a howdy-do," said Jim, covering a knowing smile with his fingertips. "Wasn't he due here at the end of the week?"

Frederick opened one eye, surveyed the situation and said, "That was my original intention, but her ladyship seems to have gotten herself into another muddle, the likes of which I felt I needed to consider first hand."

At that, Olympia shook her head and then burst out laughing. "OK, you two, what will be, will be. I'm glad you're all here, and among the three of us, we might be able to shed some light on this whole mess. And yes, Frederick, I'm delighted to see you, and no, Jim, don't even complete that thought. You will not go back to Boston, nor will you go off to a B&B for the night. I invited you to come stay with me, and it's here you shall stay."

"But …"

"Jim, as far as I'm concerned, you're family. I'll give you some earplugs if the situation should require it."

"Where do you keep them?" asked Frederick.

Before Olympia could respond, Jim took the car keys out of her hand and announced that he was going out to get some things for supper and would be gone for at least an hour.

Later, and before Jim returned, Olympia was standing in the leaky shower when she heard the bathroom door open.

"Frederick?"

"You were expecting someone else?"

"I'll be out in a minute, what do you want?"

"I want to ask you a question."

"Can't it wait until I'm out and dried off?"

"No."

"Good grief, what in the world can be so important that you have to ask me in the shower when I have soap in my eyes, and I'm soaking wet?"

"Come out, and I'll tell you."

Olympia rinsed the lather off her arms and legs, turned off the water, and pulled back the shower curtain to find Frederick kneeling on the floor holding a black velvet box in his upturned hand.

"What in hell are you …"

"Olympia Brown, I've got you cornered, and you can't escape, and I'm not going to let you change the subject. Will you marry me?"

Olympia didn't know whether to laugh or cry, so she spluttered and snuffled while Frederick continued kneeling and holding out the box.

Defeated, she wrapped herself in an oversized beach towel, sat down on the toilet and opened the box. The ring was exquisite.

"It belonged to my mother. I measured one of your rings the last time I was here, and I had this one resized when I went back to England. I'd like you to have it as a token of my affection and my intentions."

Olympia took the ring out of the box and held it up to look at it more closely. The tiny antique rose-cut diamond sparkled in the dim overhead light, and Frederick held his breath.

"Olympia?"

She placed the ring in the palm of her hand and looked into the hopeful eyes of the man she loved so much it hurt and so much that she didn't ever want to hurt him the way she herself had been hurt in the past.

"Frederick, I do love you. That much I do know. But I can't accept this if your intention is to marry me. I've seen too many wonderful relationships fall apart within the first six months of unholy matrimony. This has made me realize that I care about you far too much to risk that ever happening to us. Besides, I'm still getting to know you. Even if I were to change my mind someday and think about marriage, it's far too soon now. Can you possibly understand me and not be angry?"

Frederick sat back on his heels and looked up at Olympia. He was the picture of dejection.

"Sad, maybe, but not angry, my darling. Even if you won't agree to marry me, I'd still like to have you wear the ring. It is very precious to me, and so are you." He paused, wide-eyed. "There isn't anyone else is there?"

She shook her head. "No, sweetheart, only you."

"So whatever we agree to call this arrangement of ours, it is exclusive. Am I correct?"

Olympia nodded, and he sat up a bit straighter.

"So in the belief and reality that we are by choice the two principles in an ongoing and mutually-agreed-upon exclusive relationship, one which has no formal or legal bonds or strictures, for now anyway, will you accept and wear this ring as a token of my admiration and affection for you and my commitment to our unnamed and undefined relationship?"

Olympia looked into the eyes of the man on the floor and whispered, "Yes, Frederick, I will."

With that assurance, Frederick took the ring and placed it on her finger and then tried to get up off the floor so he might kiss the woman he loved; but in the telephone box-sized bathroom, this proved to be all but impossible. It was Jim, newly returned from his shopping trip, who heard the scuffle and discreetly knocked on the door.

"Um, everything all right in there?"

Olympia giggled and called out for Jim to open the door. When he did, he found a beatific Frederick sitting on the floor in a puddle of shower water and a teary eyed, towel-clad Olympia sitting on the john holding out her left hand.

"Hey, look at what Frederick just gave me. I think this means we're going steady."

Jim looked down at the pair of them, extended his free hand, and pulled Frederick awkwardly to his feet. In his other hand was a bottle of champagne.

"Well, I was going to leave this for the two of you to enjoy after I left, but in view of the most current development, I think I'll open it right now."

"I'll go get dressed," said a beaming Olympia.

"I'll go change my trousers while you do," said an equally blissful and soggy-bottomed Frederick.

"I picked up some Chinese food as well. It's in the kitchen."

"I'm ravenous," said Olympia.

"I'm not surprised," said Jim, "but let's start with the champagne. You've earned it."

When the very expensive bubbly was a pleasant memory and the leftover food was wrapped and stashed in the fridge, the three friends got down to the business at hand. It was a tight fit in Olympia's tiny sitting room. Olympia claimed her chair by the window, and Jim and Frederick were squeezed side-by-side on the futon by the front door. The two cats were stretched out on the fringed throw rug equidistant to the three of them. Over and above it all, on the bookshelf across from where Olympia was sitting, the antique wooden clock that didn't work remained silent.

Despite the rundown she'd given Jim earlier that day in the restaurant, Olympia decided, as much for her own sake as for Frederick's, to go over it all again, beginning with her arrival only ten days earlier. She outlined the circumstances of the flood in the house next door and her landlady's adamant insistence that she had not left the water running. Then she described finding the folder from Gingerbread Men Realty with all of Dory's information in it. Frederick then reminded her of the suspiciously loosened stair tread. And while she had no direct evidence that Dory was being pressured to sell the property, Olympia allowed as she had more than a few questions surrounding that particular issue, more so since she'd had the conversation with Dan Parker and made note of the suspicious circumstances and uncomfortable parallels related to his mother's untimely death.

"So what I need now is answers, and since I suspect that William Bateson may have some of those, I propose to start with him."

"What the hell are you talking about, Olympia?"

"You must be upset, Jim. You almost never swear."

Jim threw out his hands in frustration. "Olympia, you've just finished telling the two us that something really nasty might be going on, and much of it surrounds this William Bateson person. Now you tell us you're going to go and have a talk with him. Do you think that's wise?"

"Right now, he has no reason to think that I might be up to anything other than, as her minister, trying to help Dory sort things out. How can I possibly do that without knowing all aspects of the issue? Besides which, it's possible I might find out even more if I could make Mr. Bateson think I'm in favor of him selling Dory's house. See what I mean?"

"The lady has a point," said Frederick.

Jim peered over his glasses. "She has also been known to get herself into awkward, spell that dangerous, situations."

Olympia held up her hands in the time-out position. "Look, you two. I'm going to call the man myself. I'll tell him I'm concerned about Dory and that I agree with the daughter that the house is too big for her to continue to manage alone. Then I'll ask him to meet me at the church and tell me what his thoughts are on the matter and ask what other people do in these situations. If you think about it, while some of the happenings are definitely suspicious, we can't just jump to conclusions based on inconclusive evidence."

"The lady has yet another point," said Frederick.

Jim still looked doubtful. "OK, suppose you do manage that. Then what's going to happen?"

"I can't say until I talk to William Bateson, can I? But in the meanwhile, you, my priestly friend, will see what you can uncover about real estate scams and the elderly when you go back to Boston. With so much on computers these days and your Boston Police connections, I'm sure you can come up with far more than I ever could. Even though I'm not sure exactly what I'm looking for yet, I do know that scamming the elderly, as reprehensible as it is, is not anything new."

Jim nodded knowingly and twirled an empty wineglass in his long fingers.

"What about me? Surely there's something an eccentric Englishman can add to all of this?"

Olympia smiled at the man she had so recently confessed to loving. "Being here and being someone I can talk to about all of this is just wonderful, Frederick. When you go do back to Brookfield, continuing to work on the house that it looks like we'll be sharing is of prime importance, don't you think?"

Frederick nodded. "But I'd like to be a bit more involved, and like Jim, I'm inclined to think you could be putting yourself into a more precarious situation than you realize, Olympia. You do rush in sometimes ..."

"... where angels fear to tread," finished Jim.

Olympia set her mouth in a firm line."Look, gentlemen, a conversation in a church office with the church administrator in the next room is hardly a dangerous situation. Best case scenario, I learn he's legit but just wants to get his hands on a nice fat sale. Who could blame him for that? On the other hand, if he is up to something more underhanded, I'll sense it, proceed with caution, and if necessary call in the troops."

"What troops, Olympia? You don't know anyone here other than a few church members, and you told me yourself they don't trust newcomers. Even if you do go to the police, what are the chances of them believing you?" Jim was shaking his head in despair.

"One step at a time, Jim."

"Unless someone buggers up another stair tread," said Frederick.

"I'll be careful, I promise, said Olympia, stretching and yawning. Suddenly she was very, very tired.

"I can take a hint," said Jim. "Um, where did you say you kept those ear plugs?"

"Trust me, Jim," said Frederick, "you are not going to need them."

Twenty-Five

Olympia found William Bateson's contact information in the church directory and dialed his home number. If he was surprised that she was calling him, it was not evident in his voice or his words.

"I hope you don't mind me calling you at home, but I wondered if I could talk to you confidentially about Dory West and the condition of her house?"

"What specifically were you thinking, Olympia?" Now he sounded cautious.

"Well, as you must know, some people, including her daughter, think she should sell the house and move to a smaller place; but like so many older people, even though it's a lot of work, she wants to stay in her own home." She paused. "OK, here's the thing. I don't know enough about what the insurance adjuster was saying regarding her various options and timelines to be able to help her understand and make up her own mind. Do you see what I'm saying?"

Upon hearing this, the man sounded considerably more amenable. "I'm complimented that you'd call me, Olympia. I was getting the feeling that you were upset with me about something."

Olympia almost crossed her fingers. She hated lying. On the other hand, simply leaving some things out of a conversation wasn't lying. What was it her mother used to call it, a sin of omission? Well, she was about to commit one.

"I'm going over to the church in a few minutes. Any chance you could drop by when I'm there? If you don't mind, would you bring along that folder you left in her house, the one that I picked up last week? It's not like it's confidential anymore; we both know I opened it."

"You may have opened it, Olympia, but you did it unknowingly. I still don't think it would be ethical for me to share that information with you a second time." The cautious tone was back.

"I suppose you're right, but I've only ever bought one house in my life, and to be honest, I still don't understand everything that happened. I need a quick tutorial. Is that much within the bounds of business ethics?"

"Marginally. I'll bring the folder, but I'll keep it in my possession. Then if you have specific questions, I may or may not be able to answer them without breaking confidentiality, but I'll do what I can."

"Fair enough," said Olympia.

"Will you be there in a half-hour?" said Bateson.

"Can you make it forty-five minutes? Deb Herlihy, the church administrator, will have the place opened up by then. She's got some stuff I have to look at first."

"Does she come in every day?"

"No, just Monday, Wednesday and Thursday mornings from nine-thirty until noon. You know, mother's hours."

"I'll keep that in mind," said Bateson.

When Olympia hung up the phone, Frederick asked if she thought he should come along for ballast, but she declined, saying that a conversation in the church office with someone on the other side of the wall was hardly going to be putting herself in danger. When Jim raised a cautionary eyebrow, Olympia pooh-poohed them both, reminding them that anything suspicious thus far was a combination of circumstance and conjecture, and if she arrived with reinforcements, it might be questionable in the eyes of the beholder.

"Point," said Jim.

"Counterpoint," said Olympia.

"Pencil," said Frederick and then responded to their vacant and uncomprehending looks in his direction. "You know, something with a point."

The abstract English witticism was lost on Jim and Olympia but served to make Jim realize that Olympia knew what she was doing. "I'm going back to Dorchester this morning, Olympia," he said. "Can you drop me off at the ferry on your way to the church?"

"No problem. Are you almost ready? I told Bateson I'd meet him in forty-five minutes."

Jim pointed to a slim carry-on near the door. "I travel light."

When they were in the car, Olympia had little time to remind him to keep her informed of whatever the doctors said and ask if it was all right to tell Frederick about his medical situation.

"Eventually you can tell him, but for the time being, I need to get my own head around the situation and all of the implications before I say anything to anyone else. Do you mind?"

Olympia reached out and laid her free hand over the upturned hand of her dearest and most trusted friend. "Of course it's all right, Jim. I just want you to know there are two of us in your corner, wherever that corner is and whatever you find there."

Jim curled his fingers around hers and then smiled. "Thanks. And I'm glad you're ... going steady, if that's what you insist on calling it. It's good for you to have someone to turn to."

"I have you, Jim. That's not going to change just because I've admitted to having a boyfriend. You came first, remember."

"I got a bad report, Olympia. That does change things. Not right away maybe, but ..."

"Not another word, Jim. I'm hanging in with you for the long haul."

~

When Olympia got to the church, William Bateson was sitting in his car, waiting for her. She was comforted to see that Deb's car was in its usual spot in the shade of the maple tree that graced the lawn of the lovely old chapel. She waved, and he got out of the car. It was warm outside but not as bad as it had been the last several days. From where she stood, the clammy scent of the sea breeze coming straight off the harbor signaled a very low tide. She was already learning the unspoken language of the island. She wrinkled her nose.

"Uh huh, low tide," said Bateson, turning his face into the soft wind. "The sea gulls are feasting down by the ferry dock."

Olympia led the way into the chapel. "One of them dropped a clam on the roof of my car. Scared the bejeezus out of me."

"Me, too, the first time it happened. I know what it is now."

They were making small talk, testing the waters between them as they walked through the musty wooden building. Inside her office Olympia invited Bateson to take a chair, then pushed the door so it was almost shut but deliberately did not close it all the way.

"Where do you want to begin?" Bateson took the lead.

"I think I need to understand what Mrs. West's options are in this situation. If you aren't comfortable talking about her specifically, let's just talk about someone nameless in a similar situation, an elderly lady, living alone, whose house is getting to be too much for her and which, because of an accident, needs major repairs. As a realtor, what would you recommend?"

Bateson leaned back in his chair. "Well, that makes it a little easier for me to answer. If an adult child were living closer, I might suggest they find a place to stay, repair the house and move in together. Or I might suggest that they cut their losses, save energy, unload the place and find something easier to maintain. You know, something that's one level, or a duplex so they could have separates spaces, but something where the old lady wouldn't be alone."

Olympia winced at hearing Dory referred to as an old lady.

"Frankly, if it were my mother, I'd go for the latter. Construction is so time and energy consuming, and workmen are just so damned — excuse me, Reverend — so unreliable these days. It would take years off however many she had left."

Olympia nodded. The man was right. She continued with her questioning.

"Do you have such a place in mind or know where you might find one?'

"Not right at the moment, but if I could sit down with Mrs. West and her daughter and see where they are in all of this, I might be able to pull up something."

It all sounds so reasonable.

"Tell you what, think about what I've just said, then you go and talk to Mrs. West and her daughter. They might feel better having the first conversation with their minister. After that, if you think I might be of help, give me a call. That way you will be able to help them with what otherwise might be a difficult and emotional decision. Then you can tell me what you think is best from your perspective."

Olympia nodded thoughtfully.

Bateson blinked his eyes and sat up straight. "Wait a minute, I just thought of something. I have a friend who's an elder affairs lawyer. She has an office on the Cape and one over here. She's even given talks at some of the senior centers. If anyone knows the ins and outs of this kind of thing, it's going to be her." He flashed a warm and knowing smile at Olympia and rubbed his hands together.

Olympia nodded. "That makes perfect sense. I always say the more information, the better. You call her, and I'll have a talk with Dory and her daughter, and maybe even Julia, and find a time when they can meet with us. Then I'll get back to you. If you don't mind, I have an appointment in a few minutes, and I need to make a phone call before then."

"William Bateson almost leapt out of his chair. "Of course. I'll wait for your call." He paused. "Thank you for talking with me. I was afraid we'd gotten off on the wrong foot."

Olympia looked up at him. She was the picture of innocent wonder. "Why ever did you think that? Well, never mind, I'm glad we've cleared it up. I'll be in touch."

Olympia closed the door after him and sat alone, staring out of the window. She wasn't entirely sure the meeting had gone as she might have wished, but hearing that Bateson had a friend who was an elder affairs lawyer certainly brightened the picture. She dropped her head forward and massaged the back of her neck with her fingertips. Her muscles were far tenser than she realized.

~

Sitting in his car outside the church, William Bateson took out his cell phone and tapped in a number. "MaryAnn? It's me, Bill. You aren't going to believe this. I just enlisted the good Reverend for our side!"

~

Inside the church office Olympia was on the phone, listening to Dan Parker tell her that the autopsy report on his mother indicated that she had the heart of a fifty-year-old woman, and her cause of death was consistent with an accidental fall.

"Accident, my foot," said Dan.

"We need to talk. You going to be around later today? I'll call you back after lunch." Olympia hung up the phone and motioned for Jack Winters to come in and be seated.

~

In Olympia's cottage Frederick was picking his way around what passed for a kitchen, collecting the breakfast dishes, when he was startled by the sound of a door opening behind him.

"That you, Olympia?" He turned to see a well-dressed, slightly embarrassed looking man standing in the doorway.

"Oh, I'm sorry. I'm a member of the church. I saw the open window and thought the Reverend was home. I needed to ask her something and figured I'd save myself a trip. I'll try and catch her at the church later on," said William Bateson.

~

In Somerville, Laura Wilstrom typed David Pearlstein, Oregon, age 50-55, Northeastern University, into the search engine of her computer.

~

Father Jim Sawicki was driving north on Route 3 toward Boston, listening to the Bach "Double Violin Concerto" and weighing the relative importance and order of priority of real estate scams, medical reports … and his future life in the priesthood.

~

Jack Winters settled into the chair opposite Olympia in her office. Despite his perennial seafaring tan, his eyes showed the stress of the last several days. Olympia couldn't tell whether it was the strain of the diagnosis or the deadly cancer already manifesting itself, and she didn't really want to ask. She pushed away the awful thought and simply asked him how he was feeling and if the medical team had established a treatment program.

"To be honest, Olympia, I'm not sure how I'm feeling. Everything in my life is colored by the cancer, and that color is looking pretty dark from where I stand."

Olympia grimaced in spite of herself but was determined to sound more hopeful than she felt. "What are they going to do, and when do you start?"

"Pretty heavy duty chemo for six weeks, then a course of radiation, if I can handle it. The good news is I don't have to go all the way into Boston. I can have most of it right over in Falmouth at the hospital there."

"And after that?"

"I have a fifty-fifty chance of being impotent, incontinent or both. Isn't that just ducky? And that is only if I make it though the treatment."

Olympia shook her head in tender sympathy with the man sitting in front of her and took an optimistic leap of faith. "How long might either or both of those conditions last?"

"I guess the good news, if there is any, is that they will pass as I get my strength back." He leaned forward. "But I'm not sure I'm willing to take the chance."

"What are you talking about?" Her shock and dismay were evident in her face as well as her voice.

"Olympia. I'm a man who looks after himself. No one is going to change my diapers. I'd rather end it all now than go through that—or worse, have Janney and my sister have to witness it."

Now she was alarmed. "Jack! Don't even think that way. You've got a reasonable chance. They wouldn't have offered you treatment if you didn't. For God's sake, man, fight back. I'd be lying if I said it was going to be easy or neat, but if you have got a chance at life, don't just sit there, Jack, take it!"

"Everything all right in here?" Deb Herlihy stuck her head around the edge of the door.

"I'm sorry, Deb," said Olympia. "I get a little loud sometimes when I'm trying to make a point. I'm sorry if I alarmed you."

Deb smiled and retreated.

"What a sweetheart she is," said Olympia.

Jack looked up at Olympia. "Thanks, Reverend, I guess I needed that."

"Deal?"

"Deal." said Jack, starting to get up, but Olympia waved him back down.

"Before you go," she lowered her voice, "I want to ask you something in confidence."

Jack looked toward the open door.

Olympia shook her head. "She can't hear me over the radio. Tell me something. When I first got here, you told me you didn't trust William Bateson. Can you tell me exactly why?"

Jack Winters folded his arms. Olympia resisted the urge to count the freckles on his arms.

"I think I said he might be gay, but that's no reason not to trust someone. It's something about him. He started coming to the community church less than a year ago. When he did, he jumped right into the middle of everything. He volunteered to be an usher, he came to the potlucks and—I think I said this, too—he sucked up to the old ladies. Of course, they all loved it, but he finally seemed to settle on Dory West. She lives alone, and she ate it up. When I think about it, what's the harm in it? Some people just naturally gravitate to older people. Maybe they don't feel threatened or something. Like I said, I don't know, it's just a feeling; and since I really don't know the guy, I have no business bad-mouthing him."

"Thanks, Jack. Intuition is a wise advisor. I appreciate your candor."

"Glad to be of assistance, I think, but I really do have to be going. I'm supposed to pick up Melody in five minutes in Edgartown."

"You're not going to make it."

"No sh …" Jack stopped himself just in time, winked and let himself out.

Olympia got up and got herself a glass of water. When she returned to her desk she called Julia Scott-Norton and asked when might be a good time to meet with Dory and Jessica and William Bateson and Mary Beth Lessing, the elder affairs expert.

"I'll try and arrange it for this afternoon," said Julia. "Shall we meet here about four? That way we won't be disturbed by anyone dropping into the church, and you'll have plenty of time for lunch and anything else you might need to get out of the way."

With Jim on his way back to Boston and Frederick alone in an empty house, the thought of an extended lunch with her dearly beloved became increasingly tantalizing. Olympia could feel her temperature rising but said sweetly, "That's perfect. Dory and Jessica are already there. I'll call William Bateson and see if his lady-lawyer friend can make it. I'll only call back if they can't make it. Otherwise, I'll see you then."

When she got back to the cottage, Frederick told her about the man who had walked unannounced into the house earlier that day. He went on to say how much it upset him that someone, particularly a man, should just feel he could walk into her house without even knocking or otherwise announcing himself. But once he described what the visitor looked like, Olympia dismissed it, saying that it was undoubtedly William Bateson, and he must have thought of something after he left her at the church. This was the island, and one of the things she was learning was that not everybody knocked before they entered one another's houses.

Frederick tried to continue the protest, saying that the man, whatever his name was, had implied that he had not seen her that day. He tried to impress upon her that this was not how the English in polite society called upon one another. To emphasize his point, he firmly closed the door and locked it.

Twenty-Six

Olympia was the last person to arrive but was pleased to find someone had reserved a vintage Boston rocker just for her. Julia had thoughtfully set out pitchers of water and iced tea and a plate of oatmeal cookies on a side table in front of the window. William Bateson had spread an array of impressive looking papers on the coffee table in front of Jessica and Dory, and Mary Beth Lessing was holding up a serious looking document, explaining how it would protect Dory's holdings, both for herself and eventually for Jessica.

"Once you sign this, you give me power of attorney to work with you in whatever way you wish. I can sign checks on those days you don't feel like going out, and I can take care of legal matters so that Jessica doesn't have to fly back here every time something needs to be signed."

Dory was nodding and listening politely, but it was clear to Olympia that a lot of what was being said was going right over her head. It was late in the day, the time she usually took a little nap, and try as she might, her eyes kept glazing over.

Jessica was asking intelligent questions, but even she seemed out of her element in the face of such fluent legalese so rapidly and superbly delivered. She held up her hand to get the attention of the speaker. "OK, let me see if I understand. We give you durable power of attorney, and this empowers you to sign things like contracts, checks—in other words, whatever my mother might need while she repairs her house or waits until it's sold and uses the money to buy something that might be easier to maintain."

"I'll sign anything so long as I can go back to my own house," said Dory.

"I know that, Mum, but even if you do, that's going to take a while." Jessica reached over and patted her mother's knee.

Dory crossed her arms and stuck out her little brown chin, and Julia sent a sympathetic glance in Olympia's direction.

William Bateson cleared his throat. "Maybe I can help. From my perspective, based on the age of the house and extent of the damage, I can tell you right now that the cost to restore it is way more than the most generous settlement your insurance company will allow. Believe me, ladies, I did some checking to see what I could do. As much as you hate the idea, Dory, I really think that you should accept the settlement and let me sell the house as is. Some yuppie with a bankroll higher than his IQ would just love the job of reconstructing it. I assure you, I can get you a good price, and the sooner we get started, the better."

"Unfortunately, time is not on your side," said Mary Beth, slipping the paper on top of the others directly in front of Dory and then placing a pen on top of it. "The market is good right now. Mr. Bateson should have no problem whatsoever selling the house. I know you love the place, but I'm sure what you want, and what your daughter wants, and what even the good Reverend here wants for you is security. I know I'd want my own mother to be in a safe, secure house. Isn't that what you want, Mrs. West?"

Dory responded with a marginal nod of her head as Olympia stopped rocking and took command of the situation.

"Wait a minute, all of you. With all due respect, Ms. Lessing, I'm not comfortable with you putting words in my mouth. This is all very confusing, and I'm not in my eighties, and I have not been flooded out of my house, and I'm not being pressured to make a decision that I'm not ready to make."

Mary Beth's eyebrows went skyward. "No one is pressuring Mrs. West, I assure you. I work with elders all the time in matters such as this. The last thing we want to do is add to their confusion."

"I am not confused," said Dory.

Julia Scott-Norton turned a devastating smile toward William Bateson and Mary Beth Lessing. "I think we have enough information here to think about over the next few days, don't you, Olympia? I think what we need to do is let Jessica and her mother look at this by themselves and come to their own decisions without an audience, however well meaning we are. I can't thank you both enough for all the help you've been to all of us, but I know I never sign anything until I've slept on it, and that's what I'm going to recommend."

The meeting was over. By the set of his jaw, William Bateson was not pleased, and by her pinched lips, neither was Mary Beth Lessing; but clearly they were both too good at what they did to let it show for more than a fraction of a second.

William stood. "Of course, Julia. I'll leave everything here except the durable power of attorney. That needs to be signed on the day it's dated."

Before anyone could stay his hand, William collected the papers and shut them firmly in his briefcase. He then stepped back so that Mary Beth could stand and join him in as graceful and dignified an exit as the two could manage.

When they were outside and the door shut behind them, the elegant, well-turned-out William said, "Shit."

"That didn't go very well, and we don't have much time," said Mary Beth.

"Less time than you think," said Bateson, taking out his keys.

"What do you mean?" Mary Beth pulled open the passenger door and waited until the first blast of heat dissipated itself.

"I got word they're going to investigate the Parker business."

"That's not good."

"Like it or not, if we want to pull this off, we're going to have to be a bit more, um, proactive."

~

When Olympia returned home that evening, she related the latest chapter in the Dory West housing saga to Frederick and suggested that she should, as Julia had recommended to Dory, sleep on it before doing anything at all. When Frederick suggested that perhaps they should maybe practice sleeping before supper, Olympia smiled, shook her head and held up her cell phone.

"I just thought of something. I need to call Dan Parker about his mother's funeral service. Give me a few minutes, and then we can consider which take-out restaurant to patronize this evening."

"I could have prepared something."

"I know, and I could cook something. But right now I want cheese and grease and a large beer."

"I've got a great idea. Why don't you call it in, and I'll put on my shoes, and then if you give me clear directions, I'll go out and get it. That way you'll have a bit of privacy for your call."

Olympia smiled up gratefully. "Thanks, darling."

Frederick stood and bowed theatrically. "My dear, if I'm going to play the role of the minister's wife, discretion and all, I might as well get started don't you think?"

"The keys are in the car," was her answer.

After calling in the order and shutting the door after Frederick, Olympia called Dan Parker and asked if he had a few minutes.

"Dan, I have a question about what happened to your mother's property. Did she perchance have something in place called a limited family trust?"

"I think she called it something like that."

"I was afraid of that. Do you know the name of the person or persons who handled it for her?"

"I think I remember her talking about a man named Francis, Alden Francis. I'm at the house now, Olympia. Let me have a look, and I'll call you back at this number. It shouldn't take me very long."

Dan Parker returned the call just as Frederick came through the door, carrying a large, hot, fragrant pizza and a nice, cold six-pack. Olympia pointed to the phone in her hand, and Frederick tiptoed into the kitchen to unwrap dinner.

"I think I found it," said Dan. "It was in the folder with her will. It's a lot of legal-speak, but basically it gives full power of attorney to someone named Mary Beth Lessing and rights to sell the house to a realtor named Alden Francis of Gingerbread Realty Associates. I never heard of either one of them."

"I know the woman. Look, Dan, we need to talk. Can you come over to the church after lunch tomorrow? There's some stuff I need to check out before then, but I think your mother may have been victimized by a real estate scam that's operating right here on the island. But I don't want to say any more until I do a little more digging."

"What are you talking about?"

"I'll know more tomorrow. I hope you've got a good lawyer, because if I'm right about this, you're going to need one."

Twenty-Seven

On Friday, after she dropped Frederick off at the ferry, Olympia was enjoying a lazy morning at home. Having assured him that she had a much better handle on things now and would be okay without him until the following weekend, she had taken him to an early ferry so he could get on with his own restoration projects back in the Brookfield house. Curled in her chair by the window with both cats in her lap and a freshly made cup of coffee, she put the Parker-West situation aside long enough to consider or reconsider her own long-term options.

There was no doubt that parish ministry was appealing. While dramatically different from the academic life in terms of time and personal investment, the knowledge that she could make a difference in the lives of the people she served was a powerful enticement. She was almost to the point of getting out a pencil and paper to list the pros and cons of the idea when the phone rang. It was William Bateson, telling her that he thought he might have left his glasses at the church and asking when she was next going over there so he could come and have a look. Out of habit, Olympia shook her head, even though she was invisible to her caller.

"If I left them, they wouldn't have been on one of the seats. I remember sticking them into one of the hymnbooks. I didn't think to look when I was there the other day. That was silly. But if they are there, that's where they'd be."

"I wasn't planning on going over to the office today, but I suppose I can. It's not like it's very far. Wait a minute, don't you have a key? I thought just about everybody in the congregation had one?"

"Actually, I don't. I didn't want the responsibility. Guess it's because I'm in the business. I know what can happen."

Olympia tried to keep the reluctance out of her voice. This was one of the down sides of parish ministry. Your time really wasn't your own no matter what the contract might say. "OK, William, give me a few minutes to feed the cats and pick up the kitchen. I'll meet you there in forty-five minutes."

"Thanks, Reverend. I'm going to feel like a total fool if I find them in my car, but I looked everywhere."

Olympia chuckled. "You won't be the first or the last person to do that. I've looked all over for my glasses only to find them on top of my own head. I'll see you in a few minutes."

Bateson was already parked outside the church when Olympia pulled up behind him. Ordinarily, she would have preferred to walk the three blocks to the church, but she had decided to do a few errands and make a pastoral call as long as she was out. By the time she was out of the car, keys in hand, he was already standing on the wooden steps outside the chapel. She didn't notice the woman sitting in the back seat.

"I really appreciate this, Reverend. I suppose I could get a pair of drugstore glasses, but these are prescription glasses, and I really want to find them."

Olympia turned the key in the lock of the painted door and pushed it open. "It's not a problem. I was going out anyway." She heard the door shut and click behind them. "No need to lock it, William, we're only going to be a minute."

"Actually, I don't want us to be interrupted, Reverend."

"Wha …?" Olympia tried to turn and face the man behind her, but before she could, he pushed her forward.

"Don't say a word or make a sound. Walk straight into your office. I have a gun, and I will use it. You and I are going for a little ride up island, Reverend."

None of this was making sense. She tried again to turn and face the man behind her. "What are you talking about?"

Bateson jabbed her in the back with something hard. "Keep going, and I said don't talk. You've figured it out, haven't you? Well, Miss Do-gooder, as it turns out we are too far along in this little operation to have you screw it up. Much as I just hate to do it, I'm afraid I need to divert you, temporarily, if we can work something out, and permanently if we can't."

Olympia was totally blindsided. She couldn't believe this was happening. *Keep calm and keep him talking.* She took a deep silent breath and stepped into her office with Bateson in lockstep behind her.

"For starters, take your cell phone out of your bag, turn it off, and put it into one of the desk drawers."

When she had done that, Bateson dictated a note which read, "On emergency pastoral call," and directed her to slip it under the windshield wiper of the old Volvo she'd parked in front of the church, which by then everyone who knew her recognized as hers.

"This will keep people from wondering where you are and should keep anyone from looking for at least twenty-four hours. By then, we'll be out of here."

By now Olympia realized this was not a low budget suspense thriller but the real thing, and she was at the dead center of it. She tried to keep her voice from shaking. *Show no fear.* "Then what?"

"Like I said, if we can reach an agreement, you'll be back on the streets before anyone starts looking. I think, Reverend, you'll discover that will be the best case scenario for all concerned."

Olympia had never heard her professional title sound so ugly.

"What kind of an agreement?"

"The details of that will emerge when we get to where we can talk privately. Get into the back seat of my car. "

"But ..."

Bateson pulled open the car door and pushed Olympia forward. She ducked her head to get into the vehicle and looked into the amused eyes of Mary Beth Lessing.

"We meet again, Reverend Brown," she said, patting the seat cushion beside her, "Do get in and make yourself comfortable. It's much cooler in here with the air conditioning."

~

At the Dorchester Police headquarters, Jim had just finished explaining Olympia's situation and his research needs to his old, West End Catholic School childhood friend, Jerry O'Brien

"I think you're going to have to go into Boston HQ and start there. They've got a much more advanced research and retrieval system than we have here and people who know how to use it. We can access most of it from this office, but there's a lot of stuff that's still on paper, and frankly, I'm way out of my league when it comes to the internet. You might have to go into the BPL and go through some of the micro-files in there as well."

Jim looked quizzical. "BPL?"

"Jeez, buddy. How long you had your head in the communion wine? Boston Public Library, remember that place?"

"Sorry Jerry, I've got a lot on my plate right now."

His friend leaned forward, instantly concerned. "Anything I can help with?"

Jim shook his head. "No, not now anyway." He paused. "Church stuff, mostly."

"I know what you mean. Church stuff or cop stuff, a job's a job, and some time or other, it all hits the fan."

"You might say that," said Jim, smiling and getting out of his chair.

"Hey, call me, OK? Let me know what you find out. What is it with that minister-lady friend of yours anyway? She can get herself into the damndest pickles."

"You might say that as well. Thanks for the help, Jerry, and I will call you — promise."

~

Frederick was ensconced in Olympia's favorite chair in the sitting room of the Brookfield house. He did that when she wasn't around. He missed her and somehow felt closer to her when he occupied her habitual spot, but at the moment, the comfort zone was not working. He had just tried calling her for the third time and for as many times listened to the mechanical voice telling him that the number he called was not in service and inviting him to leave a message at the sound of the beep. This last time he did, saying only to call him at home when she got the message and reminding her of their agreement that she would leave the cell phone on whenever they were apart, and oh, yes, he loved and missed her in either order, fiercely. He missed her energy that filled whatever room she was standing in.

For some reason, the empty silence felt ominous. Olympia had assured him that the latest meeting with Dory West, her daughter, and that elder affairs lawyer, Mary Beth something-or-other, had put things in a much better perspective. If something fishy was going on, she was convinced she could handle it, but Frederick wasn't so sure. He already knew that his lady-love had a habit of thinking she could handle anything God or life sent her when, in fact, she couldn't. Then he thought about the ring she had finally accepted and wondered, even more despondently, if that too would turn out to be more than she could handle. Maybe he should call the church. Maybe she was there and would pick up.

Frederick reached for the phone just as Olympia was buckling her seat belt in the back of William Bateson's air-conditioned silver BMW.

"Where are you taking me?"

Bateson was holding the wheel with both hands and looking straight ahead. "Oh, to a charming, out of the way place I keep an eye on for some nice rich folks in Chilmark. Despite evidence to the contrary, Olympia, and you don't mind if I dispense with the Reverend crap, do you? I am a bona fide realtor, broker's license and all. I have keys to lots of places. We're going to one of those McMansions situated way back off a dirt road. The description reads: spectacular view and total privacy. The impossibly wealthy and famous owners aren't coming back until the end of September. No one will interrupt us, and if things don't work out, no one is even going to think of where to look for you."

Mary Beth spoke for the first time since they had left the church. "We're going to offer you a deal, Olympia. Basically, it's your silence or your life. Neither one of us wants to add murder to our résumé, but this isn't a time for compromise. One of our clients had an accident which proved to be fatal. It really was an accident, but it completely changes the picture. We couldn't have known the fall would kill her."

"Mary Parker."

"Clever girl." Bateson spoke over his shoulder as he turned off State road onto an unmarked and overgrown dirt road.

"What we like to do is to, um, convince an elderly client, lady or gentleman, who is in possession of a prime property that the house is getting to be too much to handle, and we are here to help. We can make life so much easier for all concerned if he or she will just let us put it into a trust or sell it, invest the profit and help the poor old dear find a smaller, more manageable place. Of course, once they sign the papers, everything is ours and we disappear."

"That's despicable," said Olympia.

Mary Beth turned in her seat. "That's one word for it; we find opportunistic sounds a little nicer. We never target poor people, just the ones with pricey properties and a family who will help them out when it all comes to light. How bad is that? Bill here knows the business, and I know the law. It works."

Bateson slowed the car and maneuvered the vehicle around to the back of the massive house. He parked it in such a way that even if a curious hiker should come rambling by, it wouldn't be seen.

"Everybody out," he said, stretching and taking a deep breath. "Lovely isn't it?"

~

Back on State Road Jack Winters cut the engine and coasted the car to a stop as far into the overgrown shoulder of the road as he could manage without actually hitting the stone wall. He eased himself out of the car, shut the door and began walking down the path, following the wheel marks of the car that had so recently turned into that very same road.

~

In the church office Frederick's voice was being recorded on the answering machine as Mike Herlihy, the church sexton and husband of the office administrator, was finishing up with his weekly maintenance chores. He thought it strange that the Reverend's car was outside with a note under the wiper saying she had a pastoral emergency and stranger still when he opened the drawer to put away some leftover bulletins and found her cell phone. None of it made sense. But she was new to the island, wasn't she? Island ways took years to learn, and Mike knew all too well that some people never did.

~

Using one of his several keys William Bateson opened the massive front door of the multilevel house and allowed Olympia and Mary Beth to pass in front of him. Had she been less terrified, Olympia might have enjoyed the breathtaking view, the massive fieldstone fireplace and the sand-colored wicker furniture arranged around a hand-woven Navaho rug on the wall over the fireplace. Everything in the room said money and reflected the colors of the view outside the window, but despite the warmth and the carelessly opulent beauty of the place, Olympia's teeth were chattering. She had been clenching her jaw to make it stop, but her face was beginning to ache.

"Sit over there."

Bateson pointed to a chair next to the fireplace. "I'll open some windows. It's stuffy in here because it's been closed. You never need air conditioning, though. There's always a breeze up here."

Olympia didn't give a damn about the view or the breeze or anything else that Bateson was prattling on about. Because of the gravity of the situation, her mind was clicking through all of the possible avenues of escape or rescue, and thus far, she had nothing on the list.

"So, Ms. Olympia, we are here because yesterday afternoon, during our meeting at Julia's place, you totally screwed up everything. We were almost there, and you scotched it. We have less than twenty-four hours to reverse that and get the whole thing signed over to us. If we can do that, then we are out of here on the next ferry, and you come out of hiding. If we can't, we go back after the daughter leaves, scare the bejeezus out of the old dear and get the house anyway. You, madam preacher-lady, are in charge of damage control, your own and little Eudora's."

Olympia clasped her hands in front of her and was twisting the ring that she had only recently agreed to wear. "Let me get this straight. It seems that a lot depends on what I do and say. Why the rush all of a sudden? The other day you said she could take her time."

"It would appear that you've poked your insistent little nose into another situation, and unfortunately, you have managed to raise a few eyebrows in our direction. We need to get out of here, but I'm not going without the West Property."

"Mary Parker."

"Precisely. It's possible you might have made a better detective than a minister, but I fear it's too late for that now. Would anyone like a glass of water?" said Bateson, walking towards an enormous, open kitchen-dining area.

"I would," said Mary Beth.

"Me, too," said Olympia. She was pleased to discover her voice was not shaking.

"Keep talking, I can hear you from here."

"To be honest," said Olympia, "I didn't think anything was going on until right now. I'll admit to having some suspicious moments over the last two weeks, but I really thought that much of the confusion was due to Dory's age and failing memory. At the very worst I thought you were just being a pushy salesman."

She hesitated, dropped both her eyes and lowered her voice. "I can be pretty oblivious sometimes. Maybe it's because I always want to think the best of people. That, and I guess I'm an instinctive mediator. I want to make sure everybody sees all sides of an issue. Up until now I was convinced that Dory was feeling pressured to sell. Jessica is concerned for the welfare of her mother, and she understands the need for her to move to a smaller place, but in the end we all know that Dory has the final word. "

William returned to the living room, balancing three glasses of water. "Well, now you know what's really going on and why we have to keep you out of the picture, at the very least until we close the deal."

Olympia felt the knot of fear in her stomach tighten. "And then what?"

"I repeat, that depends. You tell us everything you told Dory and her daughter and that super-efficient matriarch of all seasons, Julia Scott-Norton. Then you write a note to Dory and her daughter, saying you've been called away, but you've thought it over, and as her minister you are convinced that it would be best to let me dispose of the house for her, take the insurance money, and trust me and Julia to find a workable living situation for her."

"Why bring Julia into this?"

"We aren't really bringing her into it, we're just using her name to add credibility to your letter."

Olympia knew she didn't have much time. If she didn't cooperate, considering what she now knew about this operation, the picture was not good. If she told them what she knew and wrote the letter, he and Mary Beth would carry out their despicable mission. Dory would be the homeless victim of their deception. *But once they set me free, I can tell the whole story to the police and see them brought to justice. At the very least, Dory won't be physically hurt, and I get a second chance at life. On the other hand, if I don't cooperate, Dory could lose more than her house.*

Olympia took a sip of water and began to speak. When she was done, Bateson thanked her and explained that she would have to stay there under the watchful eye of Mary Beth until the papers were signed.

"But I left my car at the church. If it stays there for too long, somebody is going to get curious."

"I've already thought of that. After you sign the letter, I'm going back down island and pay a call on Mrs. West and her daughter. When I do, we'll move your car to a less conspicuous spot. Give me the keys."

"But my house keys are on the same chain."

"You won't need them."

I don't like the sound of that.

Bateson took the keys, tossed them in the air, caught them and slipped them into his pocket. Then he took a pen and a piece of church letterhead paper out of his briefcase and set it on the coffee table in front of Olympia. It read:

"Dear Dory,

Having had time to think about what was said yesterday and considering the many difficulties you will have to deal with when your daughter goes back to California and you are alone, I've come to the conclusion that the best advice I can give you is to follow William Bateson's advice and let his company put your real property and financial assets into an irrevocable limited trust to be managed by his associate, Mary Beth Lessing, Esq. I have spoken at length with Mr. Bateson, and Julia Scott-Norton, and we are convinced that this is the best option for you and Jessica. Quite frankly, the sooner it is all signed, notarized and filed with the court, the better. The money will be protected and available to you whenever you wish. If you have any questions, I can go over anything you don't understand when I return.

I wish I could be there to say this in person, but I've been called away on a pastoral emergency, and this is the best I can do for now.

Respectfully yours,

Bateson pointed to the pen on the table. "Sign it."

Olympia shook her head. "I can't sign this. If I do, she'll be homeless and penniless."

"You don't have a choice. Either you sign it, or I'll forge it and get it notarized anyway. She's seen your handwriting, but the oldies never really look. Remember, we don't want to have to ... convince her."

Defeated, Olympia signed the letter, sighed and held out the pen to Bateson.

"I feel like Judas Iscariot. I'm betraying someone I love."

"Cut the preacher crap. Look at it this way: you might just be saving her life."

With that he took the gun out of his pocket and handed it to Mary Beth.

"I can't imagine you're going to have to use this, but just in case. Remember, there's no land line and no cell phone reception up here. Once I leave, we're incommunicado, but I should be back in less than twenty-four hours."

"Then what?" Olympia was past fear now. She was helpless and furious. *Damn!*

"Then, my dear, we're going to move you to a less conspicuous spot. The only reason I'm not silencing you right now is because I may need your sweet clerical tactics to persuade dear little Dory if I can't get her away from Julia. I might need one last bargaining chip, so I'm holding onto it."

"You bastard," snarled Olympia.

"I've been called worse, but never by a minister. I guess there's a first time for everything."

And then he was gone.

Twenty-Eight

When Olympia heard the sound of the car starting behind the house, the awful reality of her situation finally sank in. This was not a bad movie, this was the real thing. There was a woman with a gun sitting across from her in an isolated mansion with a view to die for—and that's precisely what she didn't intend to do. Add to that, that dirt bag Bateson was driving off with a letter she had signed that would, if she agreed to the terms offered, leave Dory West penniless, homeless and powerless to do anything about it. Olympia was seething and becoming more agitated by the nanosecond. Wiggling her foot wasn't enough to dispel the electric tension building within her, so in desperation she got out of her chair and began pacing back and forth.

"Where do you think you're going?" Mary Beth had set the gun on the table beside her, but when Olympia stood up, she reached for it.

"Do you think I'm completely stupid? Use your head. I'm nervous, and I'm scared, and I can't sit still. Do you have a problem with me moving around? You've got the gun, and I'm about to explode. In fact, I'm not much of a drinker, but I could use one right now. Mind if I look around and see if I can scrounge up something? I'm sure there's a stash somewhere in a place like this."

Mary Beth picked up the gun and got out of the chair. "OK, but I'm going with you."

"Suit yourself."

Followed by her captor, Olympia went into the kitchen and started opening cabinet doors. Finally, in a pantry off the kitchen that was itself as big as a small sitting room, she found what she was looking for. She selected a crystal tumbler from the assortment overhead and then picked up a half-full bottle of an exceptionally fine single-malt Scotch.

"Ordinarily I drink wine, but considering the state of my nerves, I'm going to have something considerably more powerful. You want one as long as I'm pouring?"

"You surely don't think I'm going to fall for that one, do you? Get me drunk so you can escape?" Mary Beth waved her gun in Olympia's direction as if to make her point.

Olympia winced and ducked. "Do I look like I'm trying to escape? And will you for God's sake point that thing at the floor. Guns go off, you know."

"I'm quite aware of that, Reverend. That's why I have it."

Olympia poured herself a healthy double, swirled it around in the glass, sniffed at the burnt oaky aroma and then went back to the living room and stood by the fireplace.

"Aren't you going to cut that with something? That stuff's lethal."

Olympia held up her glass and looked at the amber-gold liquid. "Nope. As I said earlier, I have absolutely no prospects at the moment. You hold all the cards along with that thing on the table beside you, and I have a glass of really nice Scotch. Might as well have something I can enjoy. If I get slightly smashed, who's going to criticize me—or even care?"

"I suppose I can't argue with that."

Olympia tipped the glass to her lips, blinked a couple of times and blew out a long breath and once again began walking slowly back and forth in front of the picture window.

"You're right, it is lethal, but it's really good. I can't afford anything like this, so I might as well enjoy it while I can."

Now it was Mary Beth's turn to say, "Suit yourself."

Olympia continued pacing and sipping.

"Tell me something. Mary Parker, you did this same thing to her?"

Mary Beth leaned back in her chair and nodded. "More or less. Every case is different, but basically yes. I make the initial contacts when I offer to give a free talk at one of the local senior centers. I tell them I represent CCIEA, Cape Cod and Islands Elder Advocates, a nonprofit organization dedicated to helping seniors living on their own manage their finances. A business card and a good-looking letterhead is all I need. Nobody ever checks. People are basically trusting and lazy. There's always someone who comes up after one of my presentations asking for help. Mary Parker was one of them, and Eudora West was another."

"You mean there are more."

"We're in the business, Reverend. I'm sure that's hard for you to comprehend, but everybody has to make a living."

Olympia was having trouble taking it all in. She shook her head in disbelief. "You murdered her!"

"That really was an accident. We didn't intend for her to die. Our strategy is to gain their confidence, then arrange little incidents or accidents—or in Mrs. West's case, major inconveniences—that eventually make them realize they can't manage on their own. That's when they turn to someone they know and ask for help, and that's when we move in."

"For the kill," said Olympia.

"It's all a matter of perspective," said Mary Beth.

Glass in hand, Olympia was slowly pacing her way closer and closer to where Mary Beth was sitting. "And somebody's mother or grandmother is out on the street without a dime."

"Oh, aren't you the sanctimonious one. Don't paint it darker than it is. When I give my little talks, somebody in the audience almost always steps up, and they do because they've got money to manage and think they need help. But we made a mistake on this one. We didn't know that Mary Parker was a member of your church. That's why the push to get little Dory signed off and get out of here. We can't afford to have people putting two and two together."

"It's too late. Someone already has."

Olympia punctuated Mary Beth's instinctive look of surprise by flinging the expensive Scotch hard and fast into her wide-open eyes and making a desperate dive for the gun, but she wasn't fast enough. In what appeared to be one motion, Mary Beth grabbed for the gun, screeched in pain and pulled the trigger.

Twenty-Nine

Jack Winters had never been on this particular road before, so he didn't know how far back it went. He was making his way cautiously through the weeds and wildflowers that grew along the path when he heard a man's voice behind him.

"Stop where you are and turn around."

He couldn't believe his ears. He was out in the middle of nowhere, and he was about to be mugged. He did as he was told and almost collapsed with relief when he turned and saw a young man, far too young to be wearing a police uniform, standing in front of him. Jack noted with some alarm that the young man's left hand was hovering just above the handle of the gun resting on his hip. The name badge on his collar identified him as Jorge Tavares

Jack stepped back and involuntarily raised both hands. "Oh, man, am I glad to see you."

"I don't think I'm so glad to see you. Do you mind telling me what you are doing trespassing on what is a very private property? The owners asked us to keep an eye on the place when they're not here. Looks like it's a good thing they did. "

Jack waved both hands. "Look, I'll explain as we go. Just come with me, will you? I think a friend of mine is in serious danger."

The young officer didn't look convinced. "That's what they all say. Look, buddy, why don't you just turn around and walk back out of here with me, and we'll both forget it. Consider yourself warned, OK? Usually it's kids doing this kind of thing. Aren't you a little old to be breaking into summer houses looking for booze?"

"Oh, my God, will you for fuck's sake listen to me? I live here on the island. I have enough money to buy that goddamn house three times over. I'm not kidding. A friend of mine has just been taken in there. She's a minister. I followed her up here because I got suspicious when I saw her get into the car with the guy who was driving. Something didn't look right. It won't take you five minutes to come with me and prove me wrong, but if you don't check it out, something really bad could happen, and for all I know, maybe it already has. What do I have to do to get you to believe me?"

By the drop of his shoulders and the relaxing of his left hand, it was clear that the young man was at least going give Jack Winters the benefit of the doubt. "You go ahead of me," he said, then instinctively curled his left hand around the grip of his pistol.

The two men hadn't walked more than fifty feet when they both heard the sound of a car starting and approaching the very spot where they were standing. The young officer held his ground and motioned for the driver to stop.

William Bateson did as he was told, smiled and rolled down the window. "Yes, officer, what can I do for you? Hey, Jack Winters, what are you doing up here. Little out of your league, isn't it?"

The policeman looked confused. "You two know each other?"

"He goes to my church," said Bateson, smiling even more broadly. "Sings off key, though. I must say I'm surprised to see him up here. Jack's a harbor rat."

"He's lying," hissed Winters. "Tell him you want to check inside the house."

Officer Tavares hesitated, looking back and forth between the two men. Finally, he spoke. "Would you mind shutting off the engine and handing me your license and registration? This is a private property, and it appears you are trespassing."

Bateson was the picture of confidence and bonhomie. "I'll go you one better than that, my man. I'll give you my license and my registration and my business card. I'm a realtor, Gingerbread Men Realty, down in Oak Bluffs. I manage this property and others when the owners are off island. I was up here checking on it. Everything is in order, quiet as a church mouse in there, so you don't have to bother with it today. Now, why don't you both hop in, and I'll give you a ride back out to the road and save you some shoe leather."

The young policeman was examining Bateson's credentials when the shot rang out.

"Oh, shit," said Bateson twisting in his seat in the direction of the sound. He turned back and frantically tried to start the car. Tavares grabbed for his gun and roared, "Don't move. Turn off the engine, and get out of the car."

Then he jerked his head toward Jack Winters and said, "You too, back toward the house. You first, then the gingerbread man, then me and my gun."

"Somebody just got shot in there, you asshole!" yelled Jack.

"And I'm not going to make it a double if I can help it. Keep walking, and don't try anything funny.

As they approached the house, all three of them could hear a woman screaming. Jack Winters was the first through the door. He was greeted by the smoky, sweet smell of expensive Scotch, Olympia Brown pointing a gun in his direction, and Mary Beth Lessing doubled over in a chair, making angry cat noises and clawing at her eyes.

"Don't move," said the young policeman, pushing Jack Winters to one side and keeping his gun trained on Bateson. He looked around the room. "What the hell's going on here?"

"It think it's okay now," said Olympia, "but if I were you, I'd give the gun to Jack and handcuff Mr. Bateson. He brought me here against my will, and the woman in the chair held a gun on me until I managed to reverse the balance of power."

Bateson raised his hands in mock surrender. "Wait a minute, you've got this all wrong. I was just checking on the house. I come up here every other week. I ..."

"Shut up, you slime bag," said the Reverend Olympia Brown.

"I'm taking you in for questioning," said the policeman.

"On what charges, officer?"

"We'll start with abduction. I'm sure we'll come up with a few other charges. Turn around and put your hands behind your back."

With that, the policeman began to recite Bateson's rights, and Jack and Olympia gave each other a thumbs-up and blew out long sighs of immense relief.

Still curled in her chair, Mary Beth continued wailing and rubbing her eyes.

"Somebody get her a couple of ice cubes and wrap them in a paper towel," said Olympia. It will ease the pain and reduce the swelling. Then you'd better cuff her as well. She's part of the operation."

Mary Beth glowered through red and puffy eyes but said nothing.

When Bateson and Mary Beth had both been secured and advised of their rights, the blessed sound of an approaching siren signaled to all present that the ordeal was almost over. Olympia collapsed into the nearest chair, looking and sounding like a punctured balloon.

Thirty

After the house was secured, Officer Jorge Tavares, who had finally introduced himself by name, took full charge of the situation. He put a now silent and obviously furious William Bateson and Mary Beth Lessing in the custody of the two officers who responded to his call for a back-up. Then he directed them posthaste to the Edgartown jail where the two suspects would be held until the arraignment.

Once they were on their way, Jack offered to take Olympia back to the church to get her own car, unless, of course, she would prefer to go back to the Janney Lee and have a second chance at an oversized single-malt Scotch that she wouldn't have to use in self-defense. The lighthearted joke broke the tension, and Olympia wondered what saint she should thank for Jack's lifesaving appearance and intervention. Jack chuckled and shook his head.

"I was coming down the street when I saw you getting into Bateson's car. He has no idea what kind of a car I drive, so I slowed down and started looking around like I was a lost tourist so I could watch what was going on. Even from my car I could tell that something was wrong. You were stiff and awkward. I got a bad feeling, so I turned onto the next street, waited and then followed you. This place is so crazy in the summer, no one takes any notice of anything, least of all one more car on the road, even up here."

"That's when you called the police?"

"I never called the police. That was pure luck. Tavares was about to arrest me for trespassing. He saw the car parked in the bushes and decided to investigate. Good thing he did."

"I'll say."

"I had hell's own time convincing him to go into the house. He was trying to get me out of there when Bateson came along in the car. I was like a crazy man. I was really afraid he was going to pull it off and get away."

'What do you mean?"

"There's Bateson, the all-professional real estate agent, claiming to be on the property doing a house check. That S.O.B.'s a good actor. Tavares was just about to let him go when we all heard the gunshot, and you know the rest. Speaking of the rest, how did you get the gun away from the Lessing woman?"

"That was a last ditch effort, let me tell you. I told her I was nervous and wanted a drink, even offered to get her one. She followed me out into the kitchen, gun in hand, and watched every move I made. I eventually found myself some really high-alcohol-content Scotch, poured myself a huge glassful and pretended to drink it. I kept pacing and sipping until she was used to me walking around and finally put the gun down on the table beside her. I worked my way closer and closer, and when I thought the moment was right, I screeched and threw the Scotch in her face."

"And you grabbed the gun?"

"I wish. Even half-blind she was too fast for me. She grabbed the gun and fired it in my direction, but by then she was totally blinded and pretty well paralyzed with the booze in her eyes. That's when I got the gun."

"Pretty quick thinking for a girl." said Jack.

"Watch it!" said Olympia.

The two drove in silence for a while. Olympia was staring out of the window, trying to make sense of everything she had just witnessed, and Jack just drove, following the white line on the road and paying careful attention to the speed limit.

Finally Olympia spoke. "You saved my life, you know. Probably Dory's, too. I suppose I should thank you, but right now, words seem so totally inadequate. I mean, you really saved my life. They were very likely going to kill me. No one's ever made an attempt on my life before, and I hope to God no one ever does it again."

Jack checked the rear view mirror, signaled right, and for the second time that day pulled his car off the road and out of the traffic flow. Then he turned to Olympia and began to speak.

"Olympia, or should I say, Reverend Olympia, I've just been given a fifty-fifty chance at having a life beyond chemo and radiation. The life I've lived up until now has not been exemplary. Too much money, too much time on my hands, lots of frivolous pleasantries and one enormous hole in my life left by the death of my son. I suppose I used taking care of Janney and covering up her problems as a way not to think of my own."

"People do that," said Olympia softly.

"When we talked yesterday, I really was planning to refuse treatment and just get it over with. Today, I had the chance to do something that has made a difference, something I'm proud of. I'm thinking that if I have, in fact, saved someone's life, maybe I should give more thought to saving my own. Thanks, Reverend."

Thirty-One

When she got home, Olympia didn't know who to call first, but when she thought about it, the obvious person was Julia Scott-Norton, who could then tell Dory and Jessica. When she heard the short form of the events of the day, Julia immediately insisted that Olympia stay right where she was and allow Julia to come get her. That way, she could tell Dory and Jessica the whole story firsthand, and Julia could give her a glass of wine and follow it with some supper. If she wanted to stay the night and not be alone, she was welcome to that, too.

Olympia couldn't help but laugh. "How many bedrooms do you have in that place?"

"Enough, "said Julia.

"Give me an hour. I just need to make a couple of phone calls and see to the cats."

When she hung up the phone she looked up Dan Parker's number, then called him and gave him a quick rundown of the tumultuous and revealing events of the day. When she finished, he, too, offered dinner, but Olympia declined, asking for a rain check, perhaps sometime after his mother's funeral and before she left the island. She then asked if they could wait until after the weekend to discuss the date and details of his mother's service, if he didn't mind.

Then she called Jim, who scolded her for leaving her cell phone off but rescinded all criticism when he heard her story … and then went on to tell her his news.

"I was calling you to warn you about that Bateson person. He and the Lessing woman are the brains of an operation that has been doing this under various aliases up and down the east coast. They target areas with a large retirement community and set up shop. They haven't been stopped, because although it's a scam, the paperwork is legal. By the time the victims, or more typically their family members, start investigating, they've long gone, changed the name of their company and set up shop somewhere else. Looks like you finally tagged them."

"And damn near got myself killed in the process."

"We need to talk about that, Olympia."

"I know, look before I leap."

"Among other things. Anyway, I've got it all, and I'll get it to you. I'm sure there's going to be a trial. Sad part is, I don't think most of the victims will get anything back other than vindication that these rats have been stopped. Jail time is far too good for them."

"Well, at least Dory will keep her house, and the other one down here, Dan Parker, will get to keep his. They got greedy, couldn't resist doing it just once more, but it was too similar and too close on the heels of the other one. After listening to them, I swear to God, Jim, it was as much about the thrill of getting away with it as it was about the money."

"My policeman friend Jerry has said as much. Some criminals seem to enjoy the crime as much as the spoils. Weird, isn't it"

"What about you, Jim. Have you heard from the doctor?"

"I have. There's good news and bad news."

"Uh oh."

"Not that bad, considering. I do have to go on medication, and I absolutely have to cut back my hours. I just have to decide where to cut them. Do I stop teaching at the college, which I love, or do I cut back at St. Bart's, where I'm desperately needed?"

"Can you do a little of both?"

"That's where you come in."

"What do you mean?"

"You said I could come spend some time with you in Brookfield. Is that offer still good? I mean, I know you are impetuous and big hearted, but since you made the offer, you've accepted a ring from a very nice man. Might you not want a little privacy?"

"Oh, Jim, as a courtesy and in deference to you, I'll ask him, but I already know what his answer will be. Besides, he's so into working on that house, he's going to just love clearing out and fixing up another room. It will keep him out of mischief."

"Are you sure about that? I will have to make some arrangements for coverage. It's all still up in the air, but just knowing I have a place to go is really important to me right now."

"Jim, wherever I am, there will be a place for you. You're family, remember? Just give me a three-day warning, OK? By the way, I still haven't told Frederick what happened today, and Julia Scott-Norton is going to be here in twenty minutes. I have to feed the cats and wash my face."

Olympia's last call was to Frederick, who, upon hearing all that had transpired in the twelve hours they had been apart, insisted on returning right then and there.

"You don't have time to make the last ferry. Julia is coming to get me and has offered to let me stay the night, should I feel the need. To be honest, I don't think I do, but it's there if I need it. Why don't you take a day or two, close up the house and come down for the rest of the summer? The Jacksons across the street will keep an eye on the place. They've done it before, and they don't mind. I'll call the post office and have them forward the mail. I think it's time."

All Frederick could sputter in response was, "Jolly good!"

~

When Julia ushered Olympia into the room, Jessica and Dory both started clapping. Not to be left out of the excitement, the dog started barking and running in circles around them all. Everybody was talking at once, congratulating, consoling and asking questions until Julia took command. "I took the liberty of telling Jessica and her mother what happened, and we all think this calls for a celebratory toast. Olympia, I understand you have a fondness for single malt Scotch." In response to Olympia's dumbfounded expression, she added, "If you haven't figured it out by now, my dear, this is a very small island."

"I'd love one, said Olympia, "but just a shot with a splash of water and no ice, please. It has been a long day."

Thirty-Two

Ironically, on the day of Mary Parker's graveside ceremony the weather was about as good as it got on the Island. The temperature and humidity had dropped, and a seasoned islander would have noted a hint of fall in the color and angle of the sunlight overhead. Olympia had to take Dan's word for it as the two of them, flanked by Julia Scott-Norton and a small flotilla of lunch ladies in outrageous hats, came to bid farewell to one of their own. The service was brief but not without meaning and regret that one so vivacious and full of life was now lost to them.

When Olympia spoke the final "Amen," Dan took one of his mother's famous hats out of the tote bag he was carrying and placed it over the hole where her ashes had so recently been placed. Although no one really felt like celebrating, it was his mother's wish that they should. Accordingly, Dan bravely led the colorful group back to their cars and on to the much larger assemblage of friends and neighbors at the P.A. club where all who knew and loved Mary Parker raised more than one glass in her honor and memory.

Later that afternoon Olympia was back at the house, thinking about how in the world she was going to fit Frederick and his clothes into the place, when she heard a knock at the front door. It was Dan Parker, holding out a bouquet of flowers she remembered seeing at the gravesite.

"I hope you don't mind my dropping by unannounced, Olympia, but I don't see any reason why these should be left where they can't be enjoyed."

"Why, thank you, Dan. I was just about to have some iced tea, would you like some? We can sit on my little deck. It's gorgeous outside." Olympia took the flowers, set them on the bookcase beside the clock, and went off to get their drinks.

When they were each perched on a white plastic deck chair, glass of tea in hand, Dan was the first to speak.

"That was a beautiful service, Olympia; my mother would have loved it."

Olympia inclined her head. "Thank you, Dan. It's hard when you don't know the person, and add to that the terrible circumstances of her death ... well, I did my best."

"I suppose now isn't the time to ask, but I know you don't work for free. Can you tell me what ministers get for this sort of thing?"

Olympia chuckled. "Actually, um, how do I say this? This is part of the benefits package of church membership. Your mother was a member in good standing, if not in attendance, of the community church, and weddings, christenings, and memorial services are a benefit of belonging. There is no charge. Some people choose to make a donation to the church itself or give something like a bench or a tree in the person's memory. That would be entirely up to you."

Dan sipped his tea before responding. "You'll be pleased to know that Bateson and his buddies are all behind bars and out of commission, and my lawyer says I'm going to get the house and everything else back as it should be. It's all thanks to you. You damned near got yourself killed, you know."

"Believe me, Dan, I know. I don't mind telling you I was scared out of my mind. If Jack Winters and that young policeman hadn't shown up, no one ever would have found me."

"I'm glad they did, very glad." His voice had become husky. Olympia attributed it to his grief and sat without speaking, giving him time to compose himself.

"Olympia, how does a man who's having a glass of iced tea with the woman who just officiated at his mother's funeral ask if he can see her again ... socially?"

Olympia was blindsided but remained composed and smiling at the man sitting beside her. *What does the woman say?*

"I'm honored, Dan, but I am going to decline for two reasons. One is that, although you are not a member of this church and I am not the year-round pastor, it's still not a boundary I can cross. The second is that I have just recently agreed to an exclusive relationship with a very lovely gentleman who will be joining me tomorrow. But if either of those two conditions were not in place, then I would be delighted to accept."

He looked a bit sheepish and crestfallen. "I understand, but I had to ask. You don't mind, do you?"

"Like I said, Dan, I'm honored."

"I hope he's worthy of you."

"Let's put it this way: I've decided he's worth the investment."

Dan set down his tea and stood up. "I'll admit I'm disappointed, but I am glad you have someone nice in your life. Having said that, I really need to be getting back to the house. The police are still collecting evidence, but as of this morning, the property and finances are all back in my control, and I guess your Mrs. West is all set, as well. Is she going to fix up the house and move back in?"

"I'm not sure yet, but at least now whatever she does will be her own decision and not because of someone pressuring her. She is eighty-four, and it's a huge job, but at least she's in charge."

"You're a wonder, Reverend Lady."

"I don't know about the wonder part. Maybe that part's in the small print. But thanks, Dan, and do keep in touch."

"I will."

When she saw him to the door, she couldn't help thinking *when it rains, it pours*. Olympia had a little chuckle before setting about the more serious business of making room for the man she loved to move in.

~

With the baddies behind bars and the clean-up operation in the very capable hands of the Chilmark and Massachusetts State police, Olympia could actually get on with the business of being a parish minister. Frederick's arrival on the scene was a mixed blessing. While delighted to have him so near, having him in such proximity did present logistical problems. He was lovely, but he needed something to do besides be English and charming to the church-folk. Not surprisingly, it was Julia to the rescue.

It was not long before Frederick found himself with a considerable to-do list of minor church repairs and even some paying jobs, fixing stair treads (*Would you believe?*), changing light bulbs, and mending the fences of island residents in need of a helping hand. As a couple, Olympia and Frederick made friends with one of the Methodist ministers on the island, and the three were often seen together at summer chamber music concerts and outdoor hymn sings at the tabernacle in Oak Bluffs. But as charming and relaxed as it all was now that Olympia was no longer crime stopping, by mid-August both of them realized almost simultaneously that this wasn't real life, and it wasn't enough for either of them.

"We need to talk," said Frederick.

"I'll make the coffee," said Olympia.

"Actually, I'd prefer tea."

"I should know that by now."

When she did, the two carried their cups out onto the five-foot-by-six-foot deck and sat facing one another.

"I need my own car," said Frederick.

"Actually, my dear love, you need a life, and step one in that direction is getting your own wheels."

Frederick looked relieved. "You're not upset?"

"Why in the world should I be? This place is fairyland, at least when someone isn't aiming a gun in my direction. But we're going back to the outside world in another week, and you aren't the only one who has to get a life. I'm not a professor anymore, and after this I'm not sure that I want to serve as a parish minister either."

"So what do you think you want to do?"

Olympia shook her head. "I'm not sure, but I was thinking that a good way for me to think it over would be to do a continuing education stint as a hospital chaplain. Actually, it's called Clinical Pastoral Education, or CPE in the trade, and I can pick up some CECs for it."

"CECs?"

"Continuing education credits. I think I have enough money put aside that I can manage without a salary for almost a year. What do you think?"

"I think I get myself a green card and get a job."

"Oh, Frederick, I'm not asking you to support me.'

No, Olympia, you wouldn't. As it turns out, I'm offering."

"I have to think about that."

"No, you don't. We just agreed that I need to do more with myself than what I'm doing." He winked lasciviously. "Lovely as it is, it won't put bread on the table. So with that said, where do I find a car for myself?"

Olympia got out of her chair and went inside. She returned with that week's edition of the *Martha's Vineyard Times*. "Take a look in here. There are some unbelievable bargains here. People would rather sell stuff cheap than take it off island."

"Cheaply."

"Thank you, Mr. Grammarian."

~

Three days before Olympia and Frederick were due to leave the Island, Julia Scott-Norton called to say that the church wanted to say thank you and farewell to them both, and would they please consider themselves invited to a potluck supper on the last Sunday Olympia would be in the pulpit.

"I'm sure I can make it, Julia, but let me check with Frederick. He's out looking at a car right this minute."

"I know," said Julia.

Olympia rolled her eyes. "Julia Scott-Norton, how in the world did you know that?"

"It's a small island, Olympia, and it's my brother's truck." Olympia laughed out loud and promised to get back as soon as Frederick returned.

She was doing the dishes when Frederick returned, so she didn't hear him enter. He scared her half out of her skin when he tiptoed up and kissed the back of her neck, and her leaping screech told him so.

"Come outside, I have something to show you." The man was positively vibrating with excitement.

Olympia followed him the ten feet, seven inches, from the kitchen sink to the front door and looked out at a vintage, canary yellow Ford pickup that looked like it had been hand painted by a spider monkey using a defective roller.

"Where's the Volvo?"

"I left it back at Julia's brother's house. They wanted me to show this to you before I took possession of it. What do you think?"

"How much are they asking?"

"Tell me what you think first."

Olympia walked out to the vehicle and observed it from every possible angle. "The tires look OK. How does it feel when you drive it?"

"Well, the steering is a little loose, and the side mirror needs to be replaced, but both of those can be taken care of."

"You love it, don't you?"

Frederick nodded enthusiastically.

"Well, you won't get lost in a crowd, that's for damn sure. If you want it, then get it. It really isn't my decision. Now tell me how much."

"They gave it to me!"

"I'm not surprised," said Olympia.

Thirty-Three

On the Sunday night of Labor Day weekend, Olympia and Frederick were sitting outside in the back yard of the Brookfield house, enjoying an after dinner cup of coffee. The days were noticeably shorter now, and a lavender-pink glow was rapidly fading from the western sky.

"Such a lovely, peaceful time of day," mused Frederick.

"We won't have too many more of these. I should have brought a sweater out with me. By the way, I did tell you that I got accepted into the chaplaincy program at Mercy Hospital, didn't I? But I'm going to defer it until a little later in the year."

"You didn't, but I had no doubt that you would. I start my job at the bookstore next Tuesday."

"Well, that should be interesting. Talk about a kid in a candy store. I don't know if we have enough shelves. You might have to build some more."

"Every day with you is interesting, my darling, but if you don't mind, I think we could all use a little less excitement in the months to come. Apropos of absolutely nothing, have you heard from Jim? Do you know yet when or if he's coming to stay with us? "

"If he does, it won't be for a while. He's got a lot to think about. Oh, and another thing, I talked with my daughter Laura today. The baby's due in six weeks. She said she's doing great and feeling big."

"I suppose she's excited?"

"We all are."

"We?"

"Turns out she's scheduled to have it at Mercy Hospital in Boston, and she's invited me to be there for the birth."

Frederick reached for her hand. "Oh, that's wonderful, Olympia."

She nodded, her radiant smile saying it all.

"There's so much to be grateful for, but I'm getting chilly. I promised myself I'd get back to Miss Winslow's diary. I really neglected it while I was on Martha's Vineyard. Things sort of got away from me. So the night and the diary are mine."

As the two best friends and friendly lovers collected their cups and returned to the house, there was no mistaking the sound of silvery chimes coming from the sitting room.

"Leanna seems to be in a good mood," said Frederick.

"She should be," said Olympia, giving his bottom a friendly pat.

"Everybody's home safe. She likes it that way."

~

September 3, 1861

The end of summer is fast upon us. My garden survived my preoccupation with my child, and I have food enough to share and to store for the coming winter. My not so little Jonathan has two teeth and is already pushing himself backwards across the kitchen floor. My women friends say this is quite normal for some children. With no younger brothers or sisters, there is so much I do not know of little ones and how they grow – and no mother of my own to ask. Enough of that; there is little comfort in self-pity.

I am pondering two things with which to occupy my time and perhaps bring in a bit of money as well. I am told I have a flair for writing – and although these pages may be no proof of that, my writing was much praised when I was younger and in school. It is something I can do here at home. And in a house as big as this, with so many unoccupied rooms, I could also take in lodgers. Women of course, I don't need to raise any more eyebrows than I have already done. Since I am the sole mistress of my domain I see no reason to wait on these thoughts.

I have recently read some charming stories penned by a woman named Louisa May Alcott, and while I was in Cambridge, living with my own Aunt Louisa, I chanced upon some treatises on the education of women by a Universalist suffragist by the name of Olympia Brown. Determined to do more with my life, constrained though it might be at present, I will begin this very day by writing letters to both these women and asking their advice. Perhaps they will come to the aid of one of their own, and surely it will do no harm to ask. Courtesy alone bespeaks a response.

The days pass much more quickly now ... is it the fading sun, or is it me?

More anon, LFW

*Preview of the Fourth Olympia Brown Mystery
coming from Mainly Murder Press
October 2012*

An Unholy Mission
by Judith Campbell

Prologue

The dying woman lay on the hospital bed. Her bony jaw sagged open as her final, ragged gasps grew farther and farther apart. Her waxy skin was pale and moist, already growing cool to the touch.

On that silent night only days before Christmas, there were no family members keeping watch beside her bed, no flowers or cards on the windowsill to comfort and brighten her final days. Only a hospital chaplain stayed long past the scheduled shift, holding the patient's unresponsive hand and reading aloud from the *Bible*, easing the way with time-honored words of comfort and encouragement. "The Lord is my shepherd, I shall not want ..."

Finally, when it appeared that the woman's work of dying was finished, the solitary chaplain gently smoothed the blanket on the bed and straightened the wires and tubes still connected to the lifeless body. When all was as it should be, the chaplain closed the woman's vacant eyes and touched the wrinkled, lifeless cheek one last time. The ritual was complete. The chaplain smiled and started out of the dimly lighted room to call the nurse. *This truly is the work and will of God.*

One

Office of Chaplaincy and Pastoral Care
Mercy Hospital
Boston, Massachusetts

Dear Rev. Dr. Brown,
We are pleased to inform you that you have been accepted into our Extended Unit, Winter Chaplaincy Practicum, beginning on November 1 and continuing until February 28. This unit of study requires twenty-five hours a week of combined practical and clinical work for a total of seventeen weeks, which, when completed successfully, will qualify as a completed unit of CPE totaling four hundred hours of supervised Clinical Pastoral Education.

You are one of a highly select group of six chaplains chosen from over fifty qualified applicants. Mercy Hospital has one of the most highly rated CPE programs in the country with a tradition of excellence which you and your five cohorts will be expected to meet, if not exceed.

Please report to the Kessler Conference Room on Monday, November first, promptly at 9:00 a.m. I look forward to working with you and ask that on our first day together you be dressed appropriately, have writing materials with you, and arrive on time.

In faith and mercy,
Sr. Patrick Alphonsus, OP

When Olympia finished reading though the letter a second time, she handed it to Frederick Watkins, her live-in significant other, and began fanning herself with the empty envelope.

"That's terrific, Olympia. I know what this means to you. I think it's a good idea that you waited to be in the extended program. You must be thrilled. Think of it, you start in three weeks."

"That is one no-nonsense letter, Frederick. I know the CPE program at Mercy is rated as one of the best in the country, but this reads like an order to show up at boot camp. It doesn't sound like an invitation to become part of a religious and spiritual healing team at one of the best teaching hospitals on the east coast. It sounds more like marching orders."

~

Three weeks later Olympia Brown accepted the cup of coffee Frederick held out as she bolted past him in the direction of the sitting room. She was scrambling around the house, trying to locate her notebook and umbrella in preparation for day one of her chaplaincy program in downtown Boston; but as the relentless rain poured down outside and the kitchen clock ticked away the vanishing minutes, it seemed to Olympia that everything that could possibly go wrong was doing exactly that.

The weather was vile. Rain and high winds were predicted to last most of the day. Her ancient VW van was acting its age, and the one business suit she owned that still fit felt like someone else was wearing it.

"Is there anything I can do to help?" Frederick stood off near the sink, well out of her flight pattern.

"Other than stopping the rain, turning back the clock and getting me a new van, I don't think so, but thanks for asking, love. I still have time, but it's going to be close. I hate rushing like this, and I absolutely can't be late on the first day. It's mostly first-day jitters, I know that. I'll be a much nicer person when I get home." Olympia shook her head and smiled apologetically.

"I'll feed the cats and chill the wine. Any idea when you'll be back?"

"If this weather keeps up, God only knows. I'll give you a ring when I'm leaving. Oh, and will you call Jim Sawicki at the rectory and tell him yes to the first question, and I'll need at least a week's lead time before he does." With that she was off, head bowed against a blast of weather that belonged in a 1920s black-and-white horror film. Frederick, dear heart that he was, stood in the open doorway, waving and getting soaked until she turned out of the leaf-strewn driveway and sputtered off down the street.

The Reverend Doctor, no longer Professor, Olympia Brown was at a turning point in both her personal and professional lives, so it was not surprising that she was feeling tense and unsettled. Last May, after no end of internal debate, she had made the decision to cut her ties with the college where she'd worked for more than twenty-five years and pursue full time ministry. In that same time frame she had invited Frederick Watkins, her English gentleman, to move in and share her antique farmhouse. The house, which had a curious history of its own, was in constant need of repair and restoration and thus offered not only shelter but an ongoing salvage project the two could share in the months (and possibly years) to come.

Two major life changes in almost as many months, and a third, if she counted accepting the delicate, white gold diamond ring Frederick had held out to her while kneeling on a bathroom floor on the island of Martha's Vineyard. Even now, in the rainy gloom with almost nothing for it to reflect, the tiny flicker of light on her left hand reminded her of one more unanswered question—Frederick. She held on to the steering wheel with both hands and lurched along in first and second gears through the storm-stalled traffic on the Southeast Expressway, knowing there was no way in hell she was going to make it on time.

Olympia took pride in her own punctuality and could be less than patient with habitual latecomers. So when the combined elements of bad weather and rush hour traffic prevented her timely arrival on that first day, she was not at her professional best as she galloped toward the Kessler Conference Room.

"You must be one of the chaplains?"

Startled, Olympia caught her breath and turned to see a man carrying a black leather briefcase, hurrying to catch up with her. He was dressed in a dark suit and was wearing an imposing, hammered silver cross on a heavy chain around his neck. She had not heard him approaching.

"Y-yes, I am," said Olympia. "How could you tell?"

"I guess it takes one to know one. I'm glad somebody besides me is going to be late."

"I'm not so sure I agree with you, but my mother always used to say misery likes company. She also said there's strength in numbers, so one of those sayings is sure to apply to this situation."

The man smiled, held out his hand and fell into step close beside her.

"I'm Luther Stuart. I'm planning to be an interfaith hospice minister. And you are?"

Olympia took his hand. "I'm Olympia Brown."

When the two reached the doorway of the glass-walled conference room, Luther pulled open the door and stepped aside so she could enter ahead of him.

Right, let me go first. That way I can get the dirty looks for being late. I'm starting to dislike you already.

The other four members of the chaplaincy team, along with the Pastoral Care Supervisor, Sister Patrick, were already seated along either side of a long oval table as Olympia and Luther made their way to the two remaining seats. Sister Patrick looked down at her watch before speaking.

"You must be Olympia Brown and Luther Stuart. Come in and get settled. We're only just started." The nun paused to look around the table at the two men and four women who would be the pastoral care cohort group for the next four months. She was a solid woman, neither fat nor thin, wearing a grey, street-length jumper, a white blouse and, clipped to a headband, a shoulder-length grey veil. Olympia noted the gold wedding band on her left hand.

"Before we begin let me congratulate you one more time on your acceptance to this program. You are an elite group. As I said in your individual letters, I had over fifty applicants for this session. That means slightly fewer than one in eight were accepted." She smiled and gave them all a quick nod of approval.

"Starting today, and, in fact, beginning right now, it will be up to you to see that our longstanding tradition of excellence in faith and practice at Mercy Hospital is carried forward." Sister Patrick adjusted her glasses and sat straighter in her chair. She was a powerful and direct woman in both speech and manner, but Olympia sensed from looking into her eyes that she was also a woman of wisdom and compassion.

"You must never forget that you are dealing with human beings at their most vulnerable. You will be ministering to people who are gravely ill and, in many cases, actually dying. You will be caring for family members who are trying to come to grips with what is happening to themselves and their loved one. Sometimes even members of the medical staff will seek you out for comfort and spiritual guidance. It goes without saying, but I'll remind you anyway, that pastoral confidence is a sacred privilege. There may be times when it will feel like more than you can bear, but that particular act of trust is both the gift and the burden of our religious calling."

Sister Patrick paused for a second time and glanced across the table at Luther, who was tracing the letters on the cover of the *Bible* on the table in front of him and nodding in agreement.

"Always remember," she said, spacing her words for maximum impact, "as a hospital chaplain, you are here to serve God. You must never, ever be tempted to play God."

Coming October 2012 from Mainly Murder Press

Meet Author Judith Campbell

Rev. Dr. Judith Campbell is an ordained Unitarian Universalist minister and the author of several books and articles. She has published children's stories and poetry, as well as numerous essays on the arts, religion, and spirituality.

She holds a PhD in The Arts and Religious Studies and a Master of Arts in Fine Arts, and she offers writing workshops and spirituality retreats nationally and internationally.

When she isn't traveling and teaching, she divides her time between the island of Martha's Vineyard and Plymouth, Massachusetts. She lives with her husband, best friend and *editor par excellence*, Chris Stokes, and their two totally indulged felines, Katie and Simon.

To learn more about "The Sinister Minister" or to invite her to lead a writing workshop, preach at your church, or speak at your library or book group, please visit her website at www.judithcampbell-holymysteries.com for pictures of her marvelous cats and for some easy and yummy recipes. "Rev Judy" loves to cook, and she loves to know and talk with her readers.